"Let's say we both
week of wild, uni...

"Hypothetically, of course," Carly quickly added.

Rick nearly lost it. *Wild? Uninhibited?* Was that why she'd come to this resort? He shifted to hide his body's eager reaction, and nodded.

"Okay, then..." Carly seemed remarkably calm. "Wouldn't you want the whole thing to be anonymous?"

"Why?"

Her eyes widened. "Surely you wouldn't want anyone who knew you to be around watching."

He put up both his hands and shook his head. "Hey, I'm not into that."

She shook her head and sighed. "You know what I mean. Look, this is my one week of freedom and I'm not going to blow it."

"What do you mean? Don't you think we would hit it off in bed?"

She eyed him warily when he shifted closer. "It's not that. What part of anonymous don't you understand? I've known you for years."

Rick shook his head. She just didn't get it. "What part of chemistry don't *you* understand?" he asked, then grasped her chin and slanted his mouth over hers.

Blaze™

Dear Reader,

I'm writing this letter while sitting on a balcony surrounded by thousands of pine trees and quaking aspens, atop a mountain in central Utah. It's midsummer and the temperature is about seventy-two degrees—a far cry from the hundred degrees it usually hits at my home in Las Vegas. Tonight it will be cold enough to light a fire in the fireplace.

No wonder I fell in love with this place the first time I came here. That was a year ago May, and within two months I'd bought a condo—a refuge from the summer heat.

At the bottom of the mountain is a sleepy little town of about two thousand people—a charming place that also managed to snag a piece of my heart. A wholesome place where a Harlequin heroine could have grown up. Of course I've changed the name to protect the innocent, but this little town isn't too much unlike Oroville, the place Carly Saunders calls home. With that in mind, I started playing the "what if" game, and the result is in your hands.

I hope you enjoy my story.

Debbi Rawlins

Books by Debbi Rawlins

HARLEQUIN BLAZE
13—IN HIS WILDEST DREAMS
36—EDUCATING GINA
60—HANDS ON

ANYTHING GOES...

Debbi Rawlins

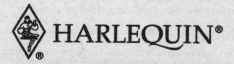

TORONTO • NEW YORK • LONDON
AMSTERDAM • PARIS • SYDNEY • HAMBURG
STOCKHOLM • ATHENS • TOKYO • MILAN • MADRID
PRAGUE • WARSAW • BUDAPEST • AUCKLAND

This is for Karl:
Thank you for lighting up my life.
I love you.

ISBN 0-373-79116-X

ANYTHING GOES...

Copyright © 2003 by Debbi Quattrone.

1

"NICE BUNS. That one's definitely an eight."

"Would you keep your voice down?" Carly Saunders slipped on her sunglasses, despite that they'd just entered the hotel lobby, and carefully avoided looking at the young man in the red Speedo.

Her friend laughed. "He didn't hear me. Besides, a guy doesn't walk around like that and not want to be noticed. Hey, check out the one with the ponytail in the yellow trunks. Another eight, wouldn't you say?"

Carly groaned. "Ginger, please do not make me regret coming on this vacation with you."

"It was your idea— Oh, my God, over there by the elevators, the blond with the ring through his right nipple. Awesome pecs. The rest of him ain't so bad either."

Obviously having heard Ginger's big mouth, the guy looked up from his magazine and smiled. Carly made an about-face and headed for the restroom they'd just passed. Ginger was going to have to check them into their room by herself.

Ginger was right—it had been Carly's idea to come to Club Nirvana, but she'd had no idea Ginger could be so brazen. Back at school she'd been a quiet, serious student with little time for dating. But the minute she'd stepped off the plane and sniffed the balmy Caribbean air, it was as if an on switch had been flipped and she had transformed into a sex-crazed madwoman.

Sure, they'd done their share of eyeing the grad-school male population. Not that the pickings were all that great at Sizemore University. Of course she and Ginger weren't exactly centerfold material either—Carly looked in the bathroom mirror and shuddered—especially not after the ten-hour flight from Salt Lake City.

She tried to flatten her spiked hair. What the heck had she been thinking getting her hair cut short last week? Changing hairstyles right before an important event was incredibly stupid.

She'd learned that when she'd foolishly dyed her hair red the day before undergraduate commencement. A few days before, Sam Black had asked her to the afterglow party following the ceremony, but after they'd all tossed their caps into the air, he'd taken one look at her rather burgundy-looking locks and she hadn't seen him since.

No great loss. He was a nerd. Just like most of her other dates. Just like her, according to some. But for now, she wouldn't think about anything but having fun and doing whatever she damn well pleased. After a week of abandon and bliss, of mindless anonymous sex, she'd return to her hometown and fulfill her promise to teach at Oroville's new middle school, total enrolment: one hundred and thirty-seven students.

"I've been looking for you." Ginger came up behind her, looked in the mirror and let out a shriek. "Why didn't you tell me my hair looked like that?"

"Like what?"

Ginger sighed. "Okay, so it's always frizzy, but you could've at least told me about this." She plucked at a particularly stubborn auburn curl that had broken free of the French braid Carly had worked on for an hour.

"Your hair is curly, not frizzy, something for which women pay good money, so get over it."

Ginger lowered her hand and stared at Carly. "What's got your panties in a twist?"

"Do you have to gawk at every guy we pass?"

"I don't gawk."

"Yeah, right." Carly turned back to the mirror. Maybe she should have gotten a few more golden highlights. Her hair still looked awfully drab, not really brown but not blond either.

"I was glancing. I don't have time to gawk. There are way too many fine-looking men here to waste time ogling just one." Ginger got out her lipstick and re-applied a coat to her already orange lips. "Do you think I should wear my pink sundress or the yellow sarong to dinner?"

Carly laughed. "We haven't been here for five minutes and you're worried about dinner wear?"

"This is a singles resort, *n'est ce pas?*"

Carly stuck her comb back into her purse, and didn't reply. She figured the question was rhetorical.

"The travel agent told us that most of the guests arrive on Friday and generally stay for a week. Today is Friday."

"And?" Carly said as they headed for the lobby.

"Tonight is crucial. Everyone will be sizing up

everyone else and starting to move in and—never mind.'' Ginger shrugged and walked out the door of the bathroom, steering toward the reception desk.

''What?''

''You don't understand what it's like to be the only girl in the senior class not to get asked to the prom.''

''Bull.''

Ginger stopped behind three women waiting in line to check in and turned to Carly with an arched brow. ''You, too? No way.''

''And how about this one? Going stag to a party and standing around while all the other girls are being asked to dance. You try to shrink into the wall pattern while you're praying that you're not the last one.'' Carly dug in her wallet for the confirmation number she'd tucked in with her blood-donor card. ''And if you get really desperate,'' she continued, ''you pretend you have to go to the bathroom, and then leave before anyone realizes you're gone. Assuming they ever do notice. Ah, here's the number.'' She slipped her wallet back into her purse, and then looked at Ginger, who stared back in surprise.

''I wouldn't believe it except you sound like one who knows.''

''I'm flattered you think otherwise. But that's the sorry truth. The only reason anyone from school would remember me at all is because our graduating class totaled sixty-three.'' Not totally true. Actually, practically everyone in town knew who she was, but only because of her father.

Ginger laughed. ''What's wrong with those boys back in Oroville?''

"Apparently the same thing as the ones in Tucson."

Ginger got serious. "I hope this week isn't a bust. I'm using all but three hundred dollars of my savings for this trip."

"I know. Me, too." Carly mentally cringed at the dismal state of her own bank account. She'd be returning to her parents' home, back to her old bedroom—she hoped without the white lace canopy bed. Expenses would be low…but the nights as exciting as dishwater.

"Next."

The woman behind the desk motioned them forward. They'd been so busy talking they hadn't noticed that the line had disappeared. Within minutes they'd registered, the bell staff had been notified to deliver their bags and they were in the elevator headed for the sixth floor.

Carly took a deep breath and told herself there was no reason to be nervous. She'd planned this trip for the past year. This was a necessary life experience. It would satisfy her curiosity, and in some ways, it would provide closure. If she ended up an old maid like her father's two sisters, at least she'd have this trip to look back on.

This week there'd be no rules. No second-guessing. No worries. She'd bask in anonymity and have the most mind-blowing sex of her life.

THE BALLROOM LOOKED like Mardi Gras in June with red, yellow and blue balloons floating around the ceiling. Others were tied to the portable bars set up in each corner of the large room, already crowded with bodies, tanned and disgustingly well-toned bodies, more bare than clothed.

Mostly twenty-somethings, Carly guessed, the ratio of men to women thankfully pretty equal. Except the women here were all beautiful, or at least confident, she noted as a blonde wearing only a micro-mini sarong asked possibly the best-looking guy in a hundred miles to dance.

The band had just finished tuning up and started playing "Night Moves." No one else was out on the dance floor yet. A few people sat at tables clustered in the back of the room, and the rest milled around the bars.

"What did I tell you?" There could be no doubt that Ginger was blatantly gawking at the passersby. And not just at the men. No discrimination here. The women wore the more mind-boggling outfits. Lots of bare midriffs and diamond-studded navels.

"Oh, my God." Ginger straightened, throwing out her chest. "He's coming this way. No, don't look."

Carly had started to follow her gaze, but instead kept her eyes trained on the stage.

"Okay, now. Look. Wait." Ginger gave her a fake smile. "Do I have lipstick on my teeth?"

Sighing, Carly shook her head. Ginger was right. This was like high school all over again. The way everyone sized each other up made her crazy.

A tall guy with a ponytail and gold hoop earring approached, and she held her breath. He passed them and asked a blonde in a slinky neon-pink dress to dance.

"His loss," Ginger whispered, and went back to scanning the crowd.

God, Carly hated this. Why did they have to have this meet-and-greet anyway? She shouldn't have come. She should have made an excuse and stayed in the room. Surely she could meet someone on the beach, or at dinner, or maybe in the bar. This set-up was too reminiscent of her past failures.

"Wanna drink?" Ginger asked, her gaze drawn to a short brunette holding a thick orange fruity concoction topped with a cherry and pineapple wedge.

"More than life itself." Carly tugged at the hem of her sundress. It hit mid-thigh, yet in here she looked modest. "I'll get them. Vodka and tonic?"

"Nah, I want one of those frou-frou ones with a paper umbrella sticking out of it. And make it a double."

Carly nodded, watching as people rapidly started to pair up. She wasn't much of a drinker, but a double sounded good about now. She headed for the nearest bar while trying to figure out how many beads the drinks would cost her.

Their vacation package was all-inclusive, with food, drinks and entertainment costs covered. But as soon as they'd checked in, they were given three strings of colored beads each to be worn around their necks and used for payment. Why they had to exchange beads for services she had no idea. Probably some sort of marketing gimmick that went over her head.

At the first bar she tried, people were lined up five deep. No one seemed to mind the wait though. They all chatted and compared tan lines, or murmured comments about the bartender's buns.

When she was finally close enough to get a look, she saw that all he wore was a red bow tie and a G-string. His partner, a blond woman who didn't even look twenty-one, wore a skimpy flesh-colored bikini top with her G-string, close enough to her own skin tone that Carly took a second look.

The entire place was about sex. The predatory looks, the sultry music, the way both the employees and guests dressed. Even the drinks had suggestive names. It was kind of fun because she didn't know anyone. Scary, too, though.

"I met you last year, didn't I?"

The voice was close to her ear, and Carly slid a look at the man standing beside her. "Me?"

He grinned. "You were here last September only your hair was longer." He made a slashing motion with his hand indicating a chin-length hairstyle.

"Sorry, wrong gal."

He frowned. "You're sure?"

"I think I'd remember being here before."

His brown eyes sparkled with laughter. "I'm sure you would."

The line moved and she edged closer to the bar, acutely aware that he'd moved up behind her. Close enough that his breath stirred her hair. He wasn't really her type. A little too muscle-bound, but he had a terrific smile. And nice eyes.

She inched into a position where she could safely turn her head and said, "I take it you're a repeat guest."

''Third year in a row.'' He already had a drink in his hand and he took a big swig. ''Great beaches, free booze, beautiful women.'' His gaze lowered insolently, and she fought a shiver. ''What's not to like about the place?''

The line moved again, giving her a graceful way out of the conversation. She gave him her back, hoping he'd take the hint that she wasn't interested. Not even ten seconds passed when she heard him ask, ''I met you here last year, right?''

She glanced back in time to see the woman behind him beam in answer. Sighing, Carly turned her attention back toward the bar.

This was what she wanted, she reminded herself. She'd purposely selected this resort because she knew it catered to singles. Heck, like everyone else here, she had every intention of getting laid this week. The affair would be anonymous, brief, and then she'd get on with her life. The guy behind her apparently had a similar agenda. He was just more open about it. Maybe she was being too picky.

It was finally her turn and she stepped up to the bar and ordered two mai tais with extra pineapple. She gave the bartender two purple beads in exchange, and then carried the drinks back to Ginger—who wasn't there. Probably in the bathroom checking her teeth for lipstick.

Carly took a sip of her mai tai, wincing at its potency. Good thing she hadn't ordered doubles. The fresh pineapple smelled heavenly and she was dying for a bite, but with both hands full, she'd be asking for trouble. She took another sip instead, feeling the stinging heat in her cheeks.

She hadn't eaten anything since she'd left Salt Lake that morning and the alcohol was doing a number on her stomach. The pineapple wouldn't be much but it would help the slight burning. If only Ginger would hurry and get back....

Carly spotted her on the dance floor. Under a spotlight, her red hair glistened as she danced to a Rod Stewart song. Her partner was a tall, long-haired guy Ginger had been eyeing earlier.

The song ended, and Carly felt annoyingly relieved. She was glad Ginger had been asked to dance, but she hated standing here by herself. The next song started and Ginger kept dancing. Sighing, Carly took another sip of her mai tai, wishing like crazy they'd grabbed something to eat as she felt the alcohol burn a path down to her stomach.

She glanced around for an empty table or somewhere to set down the drinks, and noticed a dark-haired guy staring at her. Not too tall, maybe a shade under six feet, with a wiry athletic build. She took another foolish sip and focused on the dance floor, trying to pretend she hadn't noticed him.

Ginger had really gotten into the spirit of things. Plastered up against her partner, she wiggled and writhed until Carly couldn't watch anymore. She finished her drink, clumsily bit the pineapple off the rim of her empty glass, and threw her head back to make sure she didn't lose the slippery wedge. The fruit was a little tart, but she polished it off and then started on Ginger's mai tai.

"Carly?"

She turned toward the masculine voice. It was him—the dark-haired guy who'd been staring.

He smiled. "Carly Saunders, right?"

Stunned, she nodded. "Do I know you?" She squinted at the prominent cleft in the center of his chin. Now that he was closer he did look familiar.

"You don't remember?"

Slowly, she shook her head, wondering if this was another feeble come-on. She sure hoped so. She wasn't supposed to know a soul here. Anonymity was the beauty of this vacation. A necessity, in fact.

He put a hand to his heart, laughter dancing in his hazel eyes. "After we spent two wonderful summers together? I'm deeply offended. Crushed, in fact. I'll probably never be the same."

"I think you have me mixed up with—" A flood of warm memories washed over her. "Rick?"

He grinned and held open his arms.

She could only stare. God, he'd filled out beautifully. His shoulders were so broad, his legs long and lean in his snug-fitting jeans. No wonder she hadn't recognized him. Sadly, after a dozen or so years, she obviously looked the same.

"Damn, it's good to see you. Come here."

She shifted the drink to her left hand and awkwardly extended her right one.

Ignoring it, Rick slid his arms around her and lifted her off the floor. "I can't believe it's you."

Carly tried to wiggle free. "For goodness sake, put me down."

He did just that. Slowly. Letting her body slide

down his. He stiffened suddenly, the look on his face suggesting he'd figured out that move wasn't such a good idea. "Wow, kid, you're all grown up."

Carly touched the floor and immediately stepped back. "Enough that you can stop calling me kid."

"Yeah." He pushed a hand through his hair, looking a little bemused. "What's it been, ten, eleven years?"

"More like twelve." Amazing how suddenly and vividly she remembered that last day they'd spent together. They'd watched the beavers build a dam across the stream below his grandmother's house.

Carly had reached a milestone the day before. She'd turned thirteen, become a young lady and convinced herself he'd finally return her adoration. She'd suffered her first broken heart that summer.

"I think I'd just had my sixteenth birthday that last vacation I spent at Gram's."

"That sounds about right." Carly touched his arm. "I'm sorry about your grandmother. She was a nice lady and a terrific neighbor. My mom tells me everyone in town misses her."

He shrugged. "She lived to eighty-seven in a place she loved. Can't ask for more than that."

"Sorry I missed the funeral. I was away at school and didn't hear the news until after the fact."

He shook his head. "I missed it, too. I was out of the country." His restless gaze drifted toward the dance floor. "It's noisy in here."

"Yeah," she said, torn. She wanted to suggest they go somewhere quiet and catch up. At the same time, she prayed she wouldn't see him again for the rest of the week.

Darn it. She hadn't wanted anyone to know she was here. Or know who she was. Too late. Still, it was great seeing Rick after all this time, and at least he had no more ties to Oroville. It wasn't as if he'd go blab about her to anyone in town.

"I don't really dance," he said, inclining his head toward the dance floor. "I might shuffle around to a slow number once in a while."

"No problem. I didn't expect you to ask." She shrugged. "If I wanted to dance, I would have asked you."

The corners of his mouth lifted in a slow smile. "You haven't changed."

"Sure, I have."

His gaze narrowed, and he studied her for a long awkward moment. "Come to think of it, this is about the last place I would have expected to find you."

Heat crawled up her neck. "You plied me with enough pictures of these islands. And since this is the only resort here and the idea of pitching a tent didn't cut it…"

"Yeah, I know what you mean."

"What?" She grinned. All he'd talked about for the two summers was how he was going to be a famous archeologist some day. How he was going to travel to places that no modern man had ever been. "I wouldn't have expected to find you here either. I thought you liked roughing it. Sleeping in a tent. Digging around in the dirt."

"Yeah. Right." He snorted, but seemed oddly annoyed, his gaze straying, his eyes restless. "Look, I gotta go but maybe we could meet for a drink or something later."

"Sure." Carly paused, not understanding what she'd said that was so wrong. She started to ask, but he quickly disappeared into the crowd before she could say boo.

Had his plans changed? Had he taken up another profession? No, he'd been far too passionate about archeology. Of course he'd been young, too young to etch anything in stone. Anyway, that would be no reason to be touchy.

"Who's the hunk?" Ginger came from behind, fanning herself. "Damn, I'm hot. I hope that's for me."

Carly automatically passed her the mai tai, while continuing to stare into the crowd. "His name is Rick. Rick Baxter."

"Whoa, you guys are on a last-name basis already. I thought that was a no-no."

"I know him. I mean, we didn't just meet tonight."

"No joke? How bizarre." Ginger took a huge sip and then used the damp cocktail napkin clinging to the bottom of the glass to wipe her neck. "You know him from school?"

Carly sighed. "No, from back home."

"Good God, girlfriend, you have guys who look like that living in Oroville?"

"No, he doesn't live there. He visited his grandmother for two summers. But that was over ten years ago."

"Wow! Imagine running into him here."

"He's the one who told me about this place, or at

least these islands.'' Carly smiled remembering his enthusiasm. ''He showed me stacks of snapshots he and his parents had taken. I knew then I'd come here someday.'' She lost the smile. ''I just didn't expect to run into him.''

Ginger muttered a mild curse. ''This doesn't blow things for you, does it? I mean, are you gonna be worried that he's watching you or something?''

She looked at Ginger and laughed, hysteria bubbling up inside her. Worried? She was terrified.

2

"THIS ISN'T GOING to work, girlfriend," Ginger said around a yawn as she crawled into bed.

Carly had already snuggled into her own queen-size bed. She'd brushed her teeth but hadn't washed her face. She'd regret it in the morning, but right now she didn't have the energy. It had been one heck of a long night.

"I give up," she said, her eyes closed and the covers up to her chin. she felt too tired to guess what her friend was talking about. "What isn't going to work?"

"This vacation. The whole idea of doing whatever you damn well please. You were so nervous tonight I thought I'd have to pour a couple of dozen mai tais down your throat."

"Maybe you should have," Carly murmured. It was true. After seeing Rick, she had spent a good deal of time looking over her shoulder. Jumping at the sound of every male voice that got too close.

"What are you going to do about it?" Ginger turned off the lamp at her bedside.

Welcome darkness washed over Carly. "I don't know."

"Maybe you should talk to him. You know, level with him about what you're doing here."

Carly started to laugh and then rolled over onto her side before she choked. "Yeah, right."

"I didn't mean you should tell him everything. Just that your being here isn't something you'd like broadcast."

"I don't have to worry about that. He has no reason to go to Oroville or to talk with anyone there. It's just hard knowing he could be watching me move in on some guy."

Ginger laughed. "I'd like to see that myself."

"Go ahead and joke. Your vacation hasn't been ruined."

"Oh, God, Carly, I'm sorry. I know how long you've waited for this week. There's got to be something we can do."

It wasn't as if Carly hadn't been thinking about a solution nonstop. Inevitably she'd feel self-conscious just knowing he was at the resort. Always wondering if he was watching her. Wondering if he was disappointed in her. Sure, he'd stayed in Oroville for two summers but he didn't understand the mentality of the residents. Or how it felt to be under a microscope as the town pastor's daughter.

"Carly, you still awake?"

"Yep."

"Did you and Rick ever sleep together?"

"Good grief, no. I was only thirteen the last time I saw him. I think I still believed the stork delivered me."

"Bet you had a crush on him."

"Well, yeah. He was the mysterious older man."

They both laughed, and then Ginger asked, "So what are you going to do?"

"Excellent question." Sighing, she took her frustration out by punching her pillow into shape, and then went back to staring at the ceiling. "Maybe I ought to seduce him."

"There you go."

"I was kidding."

"Why? He's hot."

Carly groaned. "He knows my parents."

"So? You just said he has no reason to go to Oroville or talk with anyone there."

"But he could."

"That's lame."

Carly rolled back over and glared into the darkness toward Ginger. "Would *you?* If a guy popped up who knew you and your parents and where you went to church and shopped for groceries, would you go for it?"

After a lengthy silence, she said, "Well, I might skip the anything goes approach..."

"Then your answer is basically no."

"I see your point."

"Thank you," Carly said tightly, so wide-awake it was pathetic.

"Carly?"

"Yeah?"

"Since you're not interested, do you mind if I have a go at him?"

Carly's eyes widened. Why should she care? Yet she had a sudden urge to pull every one of Ginger's red hairs out one by one.

WET SAND squished between Carly's toes and the sun beat down on her shoulders. She'd applied a copious amount of sun block all over her body but it wasn't really the sun's harmful rays she was worried about. Parts of her that would be exposed once she removed the sarong should never see the light of day.

"I can't do it," she said, and came to a dead stop.

Ginger took a couple of extra steps and then turned to glare at her. "Do what?"

"You know what."

"Are you still fretting over that swimsuit?"

"It's not a swimsuit. It's dental floss and two cotton balls."

Ginger groaned. "For God's sake, it's not like everyone on the island isn't wearing them."

Carly slid a sideways glance at two young women, both blondes, out of the bottle was Carly's guess, sprawled on hot-pink beach blankets only a couple of yards from the water. One lay on her stomach, and the other on her side. They both had perfect butts. Round and firm-looking, as if they worked out daily. On them the dental floss looked good.

Too good.

"I'm going back to the room and changing." She got as far as turning around before Ginger snatched hold of her arm.

"No way. That suit you brought is hideous. *I'd* be embarrassed if you wore it."

Carly gazed up at the clear blue sky and shook her

head. "I can't believe I just paid eighty bucks for this darn thing to ride up my crack."

Ginger laughed and pulled Carly along. "You'll get used to it. I promise."

"Look, if I decide not to take off the sarong, just shut up. Don't make a big deal out of it."

"Everyone else is in bikinis and you're going to sit there all covered up?"

Carly glanced down at the brief strip of material tied around her breasts and ending at the top of her thighs. "All covered up? I wear more clothes than this to bed."

"Yeah, but you usually aren't looking to get laid."

Carly's gaze darted left, then right.

"Nobody heard me. Come on. If the guys left without us, I'll be pissed."

"What do you mean left?" Carly dug in her heels. Ginger had talked her into meeting up with the guy she'd been dancing with last night. He apparently had come with two friends, both of whom, according to Ginger, were gorgeous. "I thought we were just meeting them on the beach for a drink."

"We were thinking we might go water skiing."

"You know how to water ski?"

"No, that's why I need you with me. So I won't look so bad."

"Thanks," Carly muttered. She would have been better off hanging around the lobby hoping to catch Rick. She wanted to talk to him one more time before making any rash decisions. Maybe they could work something out...have a little fun.

She was still wildly attracted to him and there was

the advantage that she knew he was safe, as far as not being weird or perverted. After a week, he'd probably be just as ready to move on as she would. Him back to his job and fast city life, and her back to Oroville.

As many downsides as there were to small-town life, she truly loved the pace, the familiarity, the safety. So she had to trade off some excitement. Heck, life *was* a tradeoff, wasn't it?

"Come on." Walking backwards as she tried to motion Carly to hurry, Ginger nearly ran into a guy with shoulder-length dark hair and orange swim trunks.

"Hold on there, sweetheart." The guy grasped Ginger's shoulders, preventing the collision.

With a startled cry, Ginger spun around. "What the—" Her voice died on the warm salty breeze when she caught sight of the hunk she'd crashed into.

Right beside him in red trunks with a smooth bare chest was Rick.

Carly's breath caught.

Carly could barely keep her eyes off Rick. She'd seen him without a shirt before, but he'd been sixteen and a little too thin. Not anymore. Holy—

"Hey, Carly." Rick smiled. "So we meet again." Without taking his gaze off her, he inclined his head toward the other guy. "This is Tony Marretti, my buddy from college. Carly's a friend from way back."

A friend. She sighed to herself. That's all he'd ever considered her, even when she'd had an impossibly mad crush on him for the entire summer.

"Nice to meet you, Tony. And the bulldozer is my friend Ginger Robbins."

The guys grinned. Ginger glared at her. But only

for a moment and then her attention was directed solely on Tony.

"You two just cruising the beach?" Tony asked, obviously interested in Ginger, as well.

"Yup," Ginger said at the same time Carly said, "No."

Seeing Rick in the flesh again brought on waves of second thoughts.

Last night under the covers in the dark it had been easy to believe they could possibly have a harmless little fling. But the way her stomach tensed and knotted just looking at him, maybe it wasn't such a hot idea.

Ginger gave her the eye—one that said she liked this opportunity better than the one they originally intended to pursue.

"By the way, I'm Rick Baxter," he said to Ginger. "An old friend of Carly's."

"Are you kidding?" Ginger grinned. "I know all about you."

Carly groaned and took her friend by the arm before she said anything she'd have to kill her for. "We have to go now. We'll see you guys later."

"Hey, wait a minute." Ginger jerked away. And took Carly's sarong with her.

Carly tried to grab it, hold the fabric in place, but the knot over her breasts untied and the sarong slid to the sand. She stooped to get it but Rick was quicker, and snatched it up. But didn't hand it over. Instead, he stared. He stared at her breasts, then roved her belly and lingered on her thighs. The look in his eyes was of raw desire and it made her so hot she thought about running for the blue Caribbean water.

But then he'd see the back of her suit. Or lack thereof. God help her.

"Thank you," she murmured and held out her hand.

His gaze narrowed as though he didn't understand, and then comprehension registered and he handed her the lime-green fabric.

"Don't put that back on," Ginger said, trying unsuccessfully to grab it. "Doesn't she look good in that bikini? You're fretting for nothing."

That did it. She *was* going to kill her. Or better yet, tell her how much redder the sun made her hair. Ignoring them all, and keeping her gaze lowered, she retied the sarong over her breasts and then tugged at the hem to cover the tops of her thighs.

Tony noisily cleared his throat. "You two want to go have a beer or something?"

"Sure." Ginger was all smiles.

Carly sighed. "Aren't you forgetting something?"

"What?"

"Justin. Didn't you promise we'd meet him?"

Ginger waved a dismissive hand. "It's too late now. By the time you had to go buy a new swimsuit and all—"

"Fine," Carly said, cutting her off before she said something Carly didn't want to hear—and didn't want the men to hear. "Let's go have a drink."

"Great." Tony took Ginger's hand. "The pool bar makes awesome pina coladas."

Rick stared at Carly, a hurt look in his eyes. "Hey, if you don't want to join us, no problem."

"I didn't say that."

Ginger stopped. "Of course she wants to come. Why wouldn't she?"

Rick's gaze stayed on Carly. "Your call."

Ginger gave her a private wink and then lifted a coy gaze to Tony. "Let's go find some shade."

"I agree." Tony gave both Rick and Carly a puzzled look before steering Ginger toward the hotel.

Carly wanted to run after them. The sudden silence between her and Rick was awkward. "Come on, let's go join them," she finally said.

"Nah, I don't think so." He threw the towel he was carrying around his neck. "I think I'll go for a walk. You go do whatever."

"Rick?" She laid a hand on his arm when he started to turn around. "I know I hesitated. It's just that I don't want to intrude on your vacation. Ginger can be a little overbearing at times. Besides, last night I got the feeling you were trying to brush me off."

"Hell, no."

"You disappeared so fast. What was I supposed to think?"

"That had nothing to do with you. Anyway, you were acting a little weird yourself. I figured you came with a jealous boyfriend or something."

"Nope. No boyfriend." She cleared her throat. "I'm just here to—" Her throat seemed to close, and she breathed in deeply.

His lips curved. "Here to what?"

She briefly closed her eyes. Was she crazy? She couldn't explain to him why she was really here—to find out what she'd been missing. Her only two sexual

experiences had been so dismal…both comedies of er-
rors—and so frustrating that curiosity was eating her
alive. Yes, modern women did it all the time. Set their
sights on a guy, made their move, but for her this
wasn't easy.

She opened her eyes and summoned all her courage.
"This is sort of a last fling for me."

His brows drew together in a puzzled frown.

"You remember how small Oroville is, and I just
finished graduate school so I'll be going back home
soon and, well…" She groaned, the heat starting to
invade her face. What the heck had she been thinking?
She couldn't do it. Not with Rick.

She'd just make the best of her vacation—get some
sun, eat and drink too much…watch everyone else
having a good time. Darn it!

"I see."

Carly caught the amusement in his eyes and her
cheeks flamed with scorching heat. She thought seri-
ously about making a run for her room. She could stay
there for the next six days and order chocolate from
room service. Lots of chocolate while she watched
television and tried not to think about what a dope she
was, and how Rick was probably still laughing his butt
off at her ineptness.

She swallowed, forcing herself not to look away. "I
don't think you understand…"

"Am I in the running?"

Her heart started to race. "For what?"

One side of his mouth lifted, and she decided it
would be better not to let him answer.

"It's just a vacation." She fidgeted with the hem

of her sarong. "Like at the end of a school year when you want to party and celebrate, except once I get home I'm going to be a working stiff, and so I—What?" she said at his knowing expression.

"You did know that this resort is a notorious pickup spot for singles."

"Really?" She was the absolute worst liar. Horrible. Even strangers knew when she was lying. "I had no idea."

Rick laughed.

"I didn't. Ginger planned the vacation." Carly knew her face was a hopeless shade of red. But she lifted her chin and stared him in the eyes.

"Take it easy. I believe you." He didn't, of course. That was clear by the way his lips twitched but she could ignore that.

"Well..." She looked around, praying for a distraction, anything that would allow her to escape gracefully. "I really don't want a drink. You go ahead and join them."

"What are you going to do?"

"Go for a swim."

"Sounds good." He looked out toward the horizon. The water was smooth and crystal clear. "I'll join you."

She groaned inwardly. "I'm really more a pool kind of gal. Salt water is bad for my hair and all that."

He grinned at her feeble excuse. "No problem. The pool is good."

"But you wanted to have a drink."

"Not really."

"Look, Rick, you don't have to baby-sit me. Ginger is free to go off and—"

Taking her hand, he pulled her close.

She drew back. "What are you doing?"

He slid her arms around his neck, and then lowered his head. Before she knew what hit her, their lips met. His felt so warm and insistent, she didn't care that they were standing in the middle of the beach with at least a dozen people around them.

He trailed the tip of his tongue across her lower lip and then over the seam, increasing the pressure until she opened to him. He tasted incredibly sweet as if he'd just sucked on a mint. His hands explored her back, followed the outline of her buttocks until he actually cupped her against him. He was already hard, his heat pressing against her belly. She wanted desperately to melt into him.

A catcall brought her to her senses.

She drew back, breathless, reluctant. Horribly embarrassed.

Rick brushed the hair away from her face. "I've wanted to do that since I was sixteen."

"Really?"

"Really."

"Why didn't you?"

"Because, kid…" He touched the tip of her nose. "You were only thirteen."

"Oh." She smiled self-consciously. He was right, of course. It didn't matter that she'd convinced her young heart she loved him. Had he kissed her, she would have run and hidden and not surfaced until he'd left at the end of summer.

"Remember how shy you were when we first met?"

She lowered her arms from around his neck, while half wishing he'd protest. He didn't. "You were the first boy I really got to know," she said. "You were totally new territory for me."

"You had a couple of school friends who hung around at the swimming hole."

"That didn't count. I grew up with them. They were just pals."

"And I wasn't?" He grinned. "I'll be damned. You did have a crush on me."

"You were the older boy from glamorous California. All the girls in town had a crush on you."

His expression got serious. "What about now?"

Her stomach lurched. "What do you mean?"

He smiled. "Has the attraction faded?"

"Well...no." She folded her arms across her chest and his gaze immediately went to her breasts. An alarming amount of cleavage showed above the sarong and she casually uncrossed her arms. "This is very weird."

"Why?"

She shrugged. "Because we have a past. I know that you hate peanut butter and jelly sandwiches and chocolate ice cream. And that you didn't learn how to ride a bike until you were eleven."

"Shit, how did you remember all that stuff?"

She peered closer. "You still have a scar."

His hand went to the side of his chin where she'd accidentally clobbered him with the butt of a fishing pole that first summer. "Yeah, you maimed me for life."

"Excuse me, but if I remember correctly I was defending myself."

"Right," he scoffed. "I think it was the other way around."

"You were trying to throw me in the lake."

"No, I wasn't."

"Bull."

His grin was slow and wicked. "Trust me, I wasn't trying to throw you in the lake."

"Then what were you doing?"

"Trying to feel you up."

That startled a laugh out of her. At thirteen she'd just started to develop breasts. "You lie."

One side of his mouth lifted. "You asked, I admitted. Deal with it."

"Gee, just as charming as ever."

His eyes glittered with humor. "We're getting off track. Why is having a past a problem?"

She sighed, wishing he hadn't gone back to that subject.

"It makes things sticky."

"That's hardly an explanation." He drew her towards him again, kissing her briefly. She breathed in the pleasant smell of the cocoa butter glistening on his tanned shoulders. "How about we go get that drink and let nature take its course?"

She almost commented on his lack of originality, but all she could think about was how much she wanted him to kiss her again. Judging by the hungry look in his eyes, it wouldn't take much to coax him.

He released her and then pulled the towel from around his neck and draped it over his arm. But not before she saw the erection he'd been trying to hide.

"Okay, we'll at least have a drink." God, she just hoped her legs still worked.

He took her hand, the feeling as natural as if he'd been doing it for a lifetime, and led her toward the hotel.

"I think the pool bar is that way," she said, pointing in the opposite direction.

Rick squeezed her hand. "We're not going to the pool. We're going to my room."

3

LITTLE, SKINNY, freckle-faced Carly Saunders. Rick shook his head as he got out the miniature bottles of booze from the small refrigerator. This was the last place he would have expected to run into her. Not that he'd given her much thought over the past eleven or twelve years.

Yeah, he'd wanted to kiss her that day they'd gone for a <u>hike</u> and picnic near Little Reservoir, but that had been hormones talking. She'd been far too young for him.

He turned around to look at her sitting on the couch. She sure wasn't now.

"Either a Bloody Mary or a screwdriver is about all we have the stuff for," he said. "Or a beer. What's your pleasure?"

She blinked, and he hoped the same thing crossed her mind as did his. "I'd rather have a soda or water."

"Even if I promise not to take advantage of you?"

She rolled her eyes at him. "Who's to say I won't take advantage of you?"

He laughed. "Sweetheart, you don't have to get me drunk. I'll do anything you want."

Carly laughed. "I'll stick with a soda."

"Coming right up." He busied himself filling a

glass with ice, coaching himself to ease up. Was she here to get laid like most of the guests? The Carly he remembered wouldn't be, but of course it had been a long time. People changed.

Amazing how he'd immediately known it was her. Especially since she looked pretty different. Most of the freckles were gone, but she had that clear fair skin that showed every hint of color when she got embarrassed.

"Here you go." He handed her a cola and sat down on the couch beside her with his beer.

She recrossed her legs so that she angled away from him.

He nudged her with a light elbow to her ribs. "You still think I have cooties?"

"I never accused you of having cooties."

"Sure you did. The first day I met you in my grandmother's backyard."

Her eyes seemed greener than he remembered, more almond-shaped. "Number one, I was only eleven. Number two, you can't remember back that far."

"Wanna bet? You climbed the fence to find a softball you'd thrown over the day before." He took a gulp of beer. "Probably just looking for an excuse to meet me."

She laughed. "I see you haven't changed."

"What?"

"Just as arrogant as ever."

"Me? No way." Having two famous parents didn't inspire confidence or arrogance.

"Please." She gave him the eye-roll again.

"You really think I was arrogant?"

Carly laughed, her sweet warm breath fanning his chin and shoulder.

"Come on, explain." Not that he cared. Right now all he could think about was what he'd glimpsed under that sarong. She sure wasn't that same skinny kid anymore.

"Don't you remember how you used to drag out all those exotic pictures of you and your parents at different archeological digs?"

"You seemed pretty impressed."

"I was. Heck, I hadn't been farther than Salt Lake City and you'd been to places I'd never heard of and couldn't even pronounce."

"How does that make me arrogant?"

She took a sip of her cola, and the way she pursed her lips around the rim of the glass had his thoughts heading due south. She'd started to relax and probably didn't realize that her sarong had puckered open a bit, giving him a great view of her flat belly and the underside of her breasts.

She set the glass aside. "Are you trying to tell me you didn't think we were all a bunch of hicks living in Oroville."

"Yeah, I probably did. But come on, I was only a kid myself. Cut me some slack."

"You asked me to explain." A smile lifted her rosy-pink lips. They were naturally that color, he seemed to recall, as if she were wearing lipstick all the time.

He took another gulp of beer. "You sure you don't want a screwdriver or something?"

"Positive. It'll make me sleepy."

His gaze went to the bed and his pulse picked up speed. "We get in that bed and it won't be to sleep."

She laughed. "Rick."

"What? You don't think I had a thing for you, too?"

"I was too young, remember?"

"You were a girl. I liked you. I had hopes." He let the back of his fingers brush her arm. "And you're not too young anymore."

She moistened her lips, and then they parted as if she were going to say something. Only nothing came out.

He smiled. "You have plans for dinner?"

Her throat worked as she swallowed. "Not really. I'll probably be eating with Ginger."

"I have a feeling Tony will be keeping her busy. He has a debilitating weakness for redheads."

"A match made in heaven. She has a weakness for nice chests." Color seeped into her cheeks. "I assume she thinks he has a nice chest," she murmured, then grabbed the cola and tipped it to her lips.

He frowned, annoyed that Carly had obviously been eyeing Tony. "I'm guessing Ginger is here for the same reason."

She arched her brows at him. "You mean, to take a vacation before starting work?"

"Don't get so defensive," he said, playfully cupping the back of her neck. Her skin was so soft and warm he wanted to run his palms all over her. Hard to believe this was the scrawny little tomboy who'd taught him how to bait a hook and beaten him at soccer. But here she was, all grown up and filled out. Soft and curvy, and making his blood simmer.

"I'm not defensive. It's just that you're making too big a deal out of a simple vacation."

"My apologies." He continued to massage her nape, pleased when she briefly closed her eyes and let her head fall forward.

His gaze followed the rise and fall of her chest, the way the rounded tops of her breasts pushed up above the sarong. The strong urge to slide his hand between the overlaps of the fabric made him sit up straighter and strategically angle his arm over his overactive crotch.

"Feel good?" he asked,

"Oh yeah." She sighed. "Too good."

"Nothing can feel too good," he whispered. He had to watch himself. Given the slightest encouragement, he'd crawl all over her. He eased up, letting his fingers trail away. "About dinner…how about we get together?"

"I don't know." She sat up straighter. "What about Ginger and Tony?"

He shouldn't have backed off. A little physical coaxing might be in order. "What about them? They can make their own plans. Or I suppose we could have dinner with them."

She hesitated, her brows drawn together in thought, her tongue slipping out to moisten her lips again and drive him insane. "This is only the first full day of vacation."

"Okay," he said slowly. "And?"

Fidgeting with the sarong, she seemed reluctant to continue. "Why are you here?"

"What do you mean?"

"You told me this was a notorious pick-up place."

"And you're assuming I'm here to get laid?"

"Yeah."

He grinned at her directness. "That would be nice."

"Okay, so don't you think you'd be better off spending your time meeting that goal?"

He didn't know whether to laugh or groan. "Talk about a brush-off."

"No, it's not."

"Basically you're telling me I'm not getting lucky here so don't waste my time."

She let out a low growl of frustration. "Don't you see? I'm letting you off the hook."

He was getting frustrated himself. "How?"

She leaned back and took a deep breath, the swell of her breasts undermining his concentration. "Let's discuss this hypothetically, okay?"

"Okay," he agreed, trying to keep a straight face. *Hypothetically. Right.*

"Let's say we both came here to have a week of wild, uninhibited sex." She quickly added, "Hypothetically, of course."

He nearly lost it then. Wild? Uninhibited? He shifted to hide his body's eager reaction, and nodded.

"Okay, then…" She seemed remarkably calm. "Wouldn't you want the whole thing to be anonymous?"

"Why?"

Her eyes widened. "Surely you wouldn't want anyone who knew you to be around watching."

He put up both hands and shook his head. "Hey, I'm not into that."

"Darn it, you know what I mean."

He grinned. "Yeah, okay, I do. But I still don't understand what you're worried about."

She shook her head and sighed. "Look, this is my one week of freedom and I'm not going to blow it."

"Don't you think we would hit it off in bed?"

"What part of anonymous don't you understand?"

"Come here."

"What?" She eyed him warily when he grasped her chin.

"What part of chemistry don't *you* understand?" He slanted his mouth over hers and teased her lips open with his tongue.

At first she tensed, but in seconds she gave up all resistance and put a hand on his chest. He deepened the kiss, sweeping the inside of her mouth, tasting, sucking, absorbing her sweetness. When her hand drifted downward, he sucked in a breath, disappointed when she stopped at his waist.

He fought against guiding her hand down to his growing erection. He'd gotten so damn hard it was uncomfortable. But he didn't want to rush her. She had enough misgivings.

Instead he drew his palm down her arm, then back up again, deliberately brushing her breast, pleased when she didn't pull away. Cautiously he molded his hand to her shoulder and then moved it to cup her breast lightly.

She whimpered softly and shifted, forcing him to lose contact. When she leaned back, her eyes were dazed. "I shouldn't be here."

"Why not?" He casually moved his hand to her thigh, while holding her gaze.

"We have to stop before it's too late."

"Too late for what?"

"To stay friends," she whispered, shifting, squirming, until his hand landed higher up on her thigh.

He couldn't tell if the action were conscious or not, but he was getting damn close to heaven. "Who says we can't?"

"This is so confusing." She sighed, leaned away and moved her leg so that her thighs clamped together. "I never ever expected to see anyone I knew here."

"But you did, and you have to realize we're two mature adults now."

"I do."

"Obviously, I'm very interested."

She blinked. "Okay, but if we do go through with this, and I'm not saying we will, we need to set ground rules."

He frowned. "Such as?"

"If we agree to a physical relationship, we both go into this knowing it's a one-week stand. Or you may decide one night is enough, someone else may catch your eye and I don't want you to be afraid to—"

"Christ, Carly, I didn't come here for the sole purpose of having sex."

"I didn't either," she said defensively.

He smiled. "I didn't think otherwise."

"Okay, then..." She cleared her throat. "You understand that this is a one-week deal, right? Then we go our separate ways.''

A disgusting thought occurred to him. "Are you getting married?''

"Married?''

"When you return to Oroville. Is there someone waiting for you? Is that what you meant by a last fling?''

"Good God, no." She shook her head vehemently. "I wouldn't be here if I were about to be married.''

"Okay. I had to ask.''

She drained her cola and stood. "Maybe I will have a Bloody Mary.''

"Help yourself." He watched her walk to the mini bar, enjoying the gentle sway of her hips, the athletic curve of her calves. "Are you still playing soccer?''

"No." She laughed. "Not for over eight years.'' She rinsed out her glass and then turned to look at him with dismay in her eyes. "This is a bad idea, isn't it?''

"Why?''

"We have a history together. Not much of one, but still…''

"Isn't that better?''

"No." She looked away and focused on making her Bloody Mary. "We can forget the whole thing, Rick. No problem. Really.''

"Just stay friends?''

"Sure.''

He couldn't tell if she was ignoring his sarcasm or just didn't get it. "We haven't seen each other in over twelve years. We've made no attempt to contact each other. I wouldn't classify us as friends.''

"I'll send you a card this Christmas."

"Very funny." He shook his head, wondering if this was commitment phobia making her so paranoid. "Is this an annual thing for you? Once a year you go on vacation and—"

She stiffened and set down the glass. Without another word, she headed for the door.

He jumped up and caught her around the waist. She shoved at his chest but he wouldn't let her go. "Come on. I wasn't being judgmental or trying to insult you. I'm simply trying to understand."

"Of course I haven't done this before. I'm just curious, okay? You know what Oroville is like. It's a darn fishbowl. I can't sneeze without everyone knowing about it."

He tightened his arms around her. She was so soft, her skin smooth and warm and her eyes... "I didn't remember your eyes being this green."

"They're kind of hazel."

"Right now they're green. Very green."

"Because I'm annoyed." With raised eyebrows, she added, "Very annoyed."

"Not at me." His mock expression of innocence made the corners of her mouth twitch.

Her lips lifted in a reluctant smile. "I don't see anyone else in the room."

"That's right." He waggled his eyebrows up and down. "We're alone."

Her gaze drew to his mouth, and he felt the tension radiate from her. "Rick, I'm very much attracted to you and I'd like for us to get together. As long as we both understand there are no strings attached."

"Ah, so you think once we've made mad passionate love I won't be able to resist your charms."

She rolled her eyes. "Don't quit your day job."

He smiled, his gaze falling to her lips. "Guess there's only one way to find out."

HAD HE SLIPPED something into her cola? Or had she simply been hanging around with Ginger too long? Carly Saunders was not that bold. Well, sometimes, but in many ways she was still that shy little girl Rick had first met, full of false bravado and bluster on the outside.

She looked away, out of the window toward the ocean. Not that she could actually see it from where she stood but she imagined the warm blue-green water gently lapping against the shore. The image did little to calm her.

"Carly?"

She wouldn't look at him, and instead reclaimed the Bloody Mary off the top of the mini-bar. He hooked a finger under her chin and brought her face around to meet his. The hunger in his eyes sent a thrill of pleasure up her spine. She forgot for a moment that she held the glass, and it tilted, the liquid sloshing on her hand and wrist

"Let me help clean that up." Then he picked up her hand and bent his head.

Mesmerized, she watched as his tongue made contact and he licked off the spilled liquid. Her breath caught at the velvet warmth of it, and she closed her eyes, knowing she should stop him, but helpless to do so.

He continued licking his way up her arm, until he got to the curve of her neck. He kissed her there and then worked his way up to her ear.

She let her head loll back. This was much better than anonymous. This was Rick. She knew him. She trusted him.

He made a low guttural sound and captured her mouth. She responded, holding nothing back, opening up to him, their tongues meeting in an erotic dance.

When his hand moved to the knot securing her sarong, she didn't stop him. When he untied it, letting it fall to the floor, and then slid his palm down the curve of her hip, she still didn't object. In fact, she did some of her own exploring, running her hand over his flat taut belly, and twirling a finger in the hair around his navel.

He was the one to finally break the kiss, his breathing ragged and heavy. "We'd be more comfortable in bed."

She swallowed, her breathing not so steady either. "God, this is so hard."

"Not as hard as I am," he whispered, lightly biting her earlobe.

"You're awful." She smiled at the casual way he ran his hand up and down her side as they talked, as if it were the most natural thing in the world.

"And you love it."

Carly bit her lip. That was the problem. She did love it. She loved Rick's irreverence, his sense of adventure, and his go-for-it attitude. She remembered how much she'd learned that first summer with him. Oh, and the fun they'd had—even though she'd gotten into more trouble than ever before in her whole life. She'd also learned that it wasn't so easy being the pastor's good daughter.

"We have to take this slow," she said firmly, straightening so he knew she meant business. "Really think about it."

"I've hardly thought about anything else."

"Rick."

The pleading in her voice must have sunk in because the amusement faded from his face. "We'll take it slow," he said as he toyed with the elastic of her bikini bottom, slipping a finger inside, stroking her skin. "Did I ever 'fess up about the dreams I had about you?"

She shook her head, his mesmerizing gaze capturing hers. "Tell me now."

He added another finger to his exploration, and yet another, and then followed the curve of her bottom, but not too far. Nothing threatening. Just enough to tease her. Make her wish he'd cup his palms over her flesh and pull her against him. Make her forget about going slow.

"I guess I wouldn't have said anything then, especially at sixteen," he said, watching her, his gaze locked onto hers. "Way too embarrassing."

Mimicking him, she traced the top of his waistband, letting her fingernails dip under the elastic, pleased at his sharp intake of breath. "I hope you're going to tell me now, since you brought it up."

"It was the typical sex-crazed sixteen-year-old boy's dream. I think I'll leave it at that."

Carly smiled. "Okay, then let's talk about what you've been doing since then."

"I thought that would be the kind of thing you would want to avoid on this vacation."

Annoyed with herself, she lowered her hands. She was curious about him, about what he'd accomplished, but he was right, getting personal led to intimacy. Exactly what she wanted to stay away from.

He shifted away and reached for his beer. "Okay, what the hell...after high school I went on to USC. Stayed for two years of graduate school. Then headed for Kenya and the Ivory Coast."

"To dig?"

"That, and to see the sights." He brought the beer to his lips, drained it and opened the small refrigerator. "What about you?"

"That's all?" She laughed, and he stared blankly at her. "Silly me. Everyone's been to Kenya. Must make for very boring conversation."

Ignoring her sarcasm, he got out another beer. "In school I did a lot of studying and an equal amount of partying. Just your average college Joe."

"You've been everywhere. That's hardly average."

He shrugged. "I haven't traveled much since. I've come here on vacation for the past three years."

She frowned. He'd been dead set on studying archeology, on making his mark in the same field as his parents. That required travel. "I'm assuming you studied archeology."

"Oh, yeah. Got my master's and all that." He gave her a pensive look. "You always wanted to teach. Is that what you're doing?"

"I will when I go back to Oroville next week. Well, in two months when the school year starts." She paused, hoping he'd continue. "You still haven't told me what you're doing."

"Trying to seduce you."

"Come on." She gave him a playful jab, but her insides were already turning to butter. "I'm serious."

He took a swig of beer, and faced her, determination and desire blatant in his eyes. "So am I. But—" He held up his hands in surrender. "We'll take it slow."

"Thank you," she said, her voice a breathless betrayal. "Let's talk some more."

"Oh, brother."

She ignored his grumpy expression. "How are your parents?"

"Divorced."

"You're kidding."

"Why the surprise? It happens to couples all the time."

"So they don't work together anymore?"

He gave her a mocking look. "That's about the only thing they could do together without fighting."

"I didn't know," she murmured. As a boy he'd told a different story. To him they were like gods.

"No big deal." He set down the beer. "If we're going to talk, sweetheart, it's not going to be about the past." And then he reached for her. "Let's talk about what we're going to do tonight...."

4

"IN CASE you've forgotten, this room has only one bathroom." Disgusted, Carly pounded on the door for the third time. The lighting at the desk was too dim and she had only five minutes left to finish applying her makeup.

"Hold on." Ginger's impatient tone only made Carly more annoyed. "This humidity is doing a number on my hair."

"Your frizzy hair will be the least of your worries if you don't open this darn door."

It opened suddenly. Ginger frowned at her. "What the hell has gotten into you?"

"We have only five minutes before we meet the guys for dinner." Carly jabbed a finger at her watch. "You can do your hair out here. I need the bathroom light for my makeup."

"No kidding. You look like a clown." Ginger threw her a cool look as she pushed past, curling iron in hand.

Tempted to make a crack about her frizzy hair, Carly held her tongue. Ginger always hogged the bathroom and Carly seldom minded. But this evening she was in a strange mood. Edgy. Uncertain. Scared to death.

It was only dinner, she told herself as she set down her makeup bag, looked in the mirror and sighed. She did look like a clown. Too much blush. The unfortunate bluish eye shadow made her look eerily like her mother's high-school graduation picture.

She loved her mom, but yuk... Carly was used to wearing a more natural shade when she bothered at all. So why was she making herself crazy? She knew in her heart that Rick wasn't a candidate for her week of therapeutic debauchery. No, actually she knew intellectually he wasn't the right one. Her heart foolishly wanted to jump in head-first.

"What are you scrubbing all that off for?" Ginger stared at her from the doorway. "Shit, I'm sorry. I didn't mean it about you looking like a clown."

"You were right. This isn't me."

"It's going to be dark. You'll want to wear more makeup than usual."

"Mascara and blush will be enough."

Ginger sighed. "Yeah, I guess he's pretty much a sure thing."

Carly slid her a sidelong glance. "What do you mean?"

"I saw the way Rick looked at you."

"We're friends. That's all." Carly turned back to the mirror and inspected her bald face before reapplying the tinted moisturizer.

"Friends?" Ginger chuckled. "Okay, but don't tell me you're not ready to jump his bones."

"I am most certainly not ready to jump his bones. I haven't decided yet." Carly smoothed in some foundation to blot out several obnoxious freckles. "Are you ready?"

"Pretty much." She reached around Carly for the hairspray. "I don't understand you. The guy is gorgeous. He obviously wants you. You've been doing a little drooling yourself. What's the problem?"

"You have to ask? This whole week was supposed to be about anonymity."

"So? Isn't it better that you know and like him, and who knows what could develop? You said yourself you'd eventually like to get married."

"Nothing can develop. That's the—" Carly cut herself short. She didn't want to get into this discussion with Ginger. Or anyone. It was too hard to explain. Her longings were a mystery even to herself.

Yes, she eventually wanted to have a husband, start a family, and she wanted to do it in Oroville. She loved her home, and she wanted her children to have the same advantages she'd had growing up in a small loving community. The problem was, the guys who lived there were conservative and boring, with not much more ambition than to own a new pickup every three years.

Not like Rick. He'd been exciting and adventurous and had brought out a reckless streak in her she hadn't known she possessed. The discovery had been both exhilarating and scary, and the careless behavior not always easy to suppress.

Even now she could clearly recall the time he'd suggested they explore the old Colby mine. Condemned since she'd learned how to talk, the mine had been strictly off limits and all the kids in Oroville knew it.

None of them would even dream about ignoring the no trespassing sign. But all he'd had had to do was dare her...

She smiled. That was one of her best afternoons ever.

Darn it. She could *really* like Rick. Heck, she already did. But, at this point, it wasn't like she'd go home and pine away for him. Intimacy could change that. Then where would she be?

"Damn it. Look at the time. We're late." Ginger squeezed her eyes shut and aimed the hairspray at her French braid.

Spray went everywhere, and Carly grabbed her makeup bag and exited the bathroom in a fit of coughing. She applied some blush with a far lighter touch this time and decided to forgo any eye pencil.

"Okay." Ginger surfaced from the bathroom, and slung her purse over her shoulder. "Ready for action." She adjusted the top of her turquoise sundress to get maximum cleavage. "I'm talking really ready." She grinned. "Tony isn't going to know what hit him."

Carly laughed as she grabbed her own purse. She couldn't help it. What a piece of work. "I don't think you'll have to worry about coercing Tony."

Ginger got to the door but stopped, her eyes sparkling. "Why? Did Rick say something?"

"Oh, please. He didn't have to." Carly made a shooing motion, trying to get her friend out the door. "Tony is definitely hot for you."

A pleased smile curved Ginger's lips as she walked

out into the corridor. "I'm betting he just might get lucky tonight."

"Might?" Carly pulled the door closed. "Yeah, right."

Ginger laughed. "Which reminds me. How are we going to work the room thing?"

Carly frowned at first, and then she got it, petty envy taking a bite out of her. "Just put out the do not disturb sign and I'll disappear for a while."

"If he spends the night with me, you can spend it with Rick in their room, right?"

Carly swallowed her disappointment and jealousy. "Sure," she said, ignoring the butterflies that had turned her stomach into a circus.

"WHAT LOOKS GOOD?" Tony stared at the menu. "Anybody ever have conch chowder?"

Carly had never even heard of the dish. She glanced at Ginger who was too busy making goo-goo eyes at Tony to notice.

"It's okay," Rick said. "I prefer abalone myself, but it's a local favorite. You ought to try it once while we're here."

"You're right. Try everything once is my motto." Tony grinned at Ginger. "Go back for seconds if you like it."

She giggled and gave his arm a playful punch.

Carly started to roll her eyes but caught herself. From her peripheral vision, she saw Rick watching her. Instead of acknowledging him, she buried her nose in the menu.

"What are you having, Carly?" He touched her

hand and she jerked in surprise, nearly knocking over the pina colada he'd ordered for her before she and Ginger had arrived.

She set down the menu and clasped her hands in her lap. "I'm not sure."

"Want me to make a couple of suggestions?"

Something in his lowered voice made her look up. He winked and her silly heart fluttered. "I'll probably have the mango chicken."

"Oysters," Tony suggested. "They're good for—"

Giggling, Ginger nudged him again. "We all know what they're good for." With a lift of her chin, she made a teasing sound of disgust. "As if I need an aphrodisiac."

Tony smiled and whispered something in her ear.

Carly inwardly groaned and quickly picked up the menu again. Why on earth had she agreed to come to dinner with them? Stupid question. She wasn't ready to be alone with Rick again.

"Come on, children, save this for later." Rick threw a wadded up cocktail napkin at Tony.

"We have far more interesting matters to discuss later," Tony said, throwing the napkin back and giving Ginger a significant look.

Thankfully, Tony and Ginger cooled it long enough to order and eat dinner. Carly knew Rick had spoken up because he noticed she was embarrassed. Not embarrassed, really, more uncomfortable. And a little annoyed. Not with Ginger or Tony, certainly not with Rick, but with the situation in general.

She'd loved flirting with him earlier. No way could she deny the incredible chemistry that had made the entire room sizzle. She'd relived the touching and kissing the rest of the afternoon, but in the end apprehension nailed her. If she did anything with Rick, she was going to think back to it forever and ever. Think about the carefree person she was with him, and about what could have been. Sad, but true.

Which left her starting to panic over her vacation. How could she possibly enjoy herself wondering if he was watching her? She would have to think of something quickly or spend the rest of the week watching reruns of *Buffy the Vampire Slayer*.

She blinked at the stunning blond waitress who smiled at Rick as she served them another round of pina coladas. Maybe the week was still salvageable, after all. If Rick hooked up with someone, he'd be too busy to pay attention to what Carly was doing....

The sudden thought stirred mixed emotions. Jealousy clawed at her just thinking about him being with another woman. Ridiculous, of course, but there it was. Yet there was also relief in knowing she wouldn't have to look over her shoulder constantly.

"Would you like anything else?" the blond waitress asked them, although her attention was mostly directed at Rick.

"I'm fine," he said. "What about the rest of you? Want some dessert?"

Tony and Ginger promptly shook their heads. No big surprise. They were clearly anxious to be off on their own.

"Okay, I guess that's it." Rick reached into his pocket. "How many beads do I owe you?"

"I'd like some dessert," Carly said.

Tony and Ginger had already gotten up from the table, but they hesitated.

"Go ahead." She waved them off. "Rick will keep me company, won't you?"

"Of course."

"Okay, we'll see you guys later." Tony exchanged a knowing look with Rick, and then steered Ginger toward the door.

"Would you like to see the menu again?" the waitress asked, perky and braless beneath her pink T-shirt.

Rick had given her a couple of glances, but nothing more than Carly herself had done. The woman's brief white shorts showed an extraordinary amount of well-defined leg as she leaned across the table to remove dishes, but, again, Rick didn't seem overly interested.

Carly shook her head. "I know what I want. A hot fudge sundae with extra whipped cream."

Rick chuckled, one eyebrow lifting in surprise. "Better make that two," he said to the waitress, his gaze staying on Carly.

"Coming right up." The blonde picked up a couple of more plates and then drifted to the next table.

Still, Rick's interest remained solely on Carly. She felt a stupid thrill that she could hold his rapt attention. Which was crazy. She was supposed to be trying to get rid of him.

"I need help trying to figure something out here." Rick pursed his lips, looking suspiciously as if he were trying not to laugh.

"Yes?" She forced herself to hold his gaze.

"Why you're stalling."

"That's ridiculous."

"Either you're thinking of a way to get rid of me, or figuring out how to get me in the sack. Which of course would be a no-brainer."

"Why does this have to be about you?" Carly bristled and didn't care that it showed. "I simply would like a hot fudge sundae, okay?"

He laughed. "Okay."

Anxious to busy herself, she started digging in her purse for her beads. And then she realized that, like a good girl, she'd put them around her neck, just as they'd instructed her to do at check-in. "How much do I owe you for dinner?"

"Forget it."

She removed a string from around her neck. "No, we all were given a certain allotment of beads, and it wouldn't be fair for you to run out."

"You can pay the tab next time."

"What if there isn't a next time?"

He narrowed his gaze and studied her face.

The silence grew uncomfortable, and she stared down at the cocktail napkin she'd been shredding. "You know, you might hook up with someone else and I won't see much of you."

"Carly," he said, as if scolding a child, and then he took the string of beads out of her other hand, "I thought we'd already settled that."

She slid a glance at the beads, wondering what he had planned for them. He leaned close and then slipped them over her head and kissed her briefly on the lips. He pulled back slightly to smile at her.

"Here you go." The waitress appeared with their sundaes. "I put extra whipped cream on both," she said as she set a huge glass bowl in front of each of them.

"Thanks," Carly said.

The server smiled. "Anything else?"

Rick raised a questioning brow at Carly. She shook her head and picked up her spoon, no longer interested in dessert. What she wanted was for Rick to kiss her again.

She also wanted him to go away and leave her alone.

What a mess.

The waitress gave Rick the total, and he dropped the appropriate number of beads in her hand. Although she remained pleasant, she didn't seem nearly as interested in Rick as before, and Carly realized the kiss must have warned her off.

Foolish pleasure warmed her, and when Rick dipped his spoon into his sundae and brought the offering to her lips, she didn't hesitate. He smiled and brushed some stray whipped cream off her top lip. She had the nearly irresistible urge to draw his thumb into her mouth. She stopped herself, but when she met his gaze she knew she was busted.

He knew how turned on she was. It was there in the golden flecks in his eyes, like liquid flames of desire, matching her own wants and needs.

God, she wanted him. Wanted to go back to her room and strip him naked. Explore every nuance of his body. What would be so terrible about being with Rick? She couldn't possibly get too attached in just one week, could she? And then she'd never see him again. Equally important, he had no reason to go to Oroville.

"After we finish, let's go for a walk on the beach," Rick whispered, using the tip of his finger to draw abstract patterns on the back of her hand.

She polished off the gooey ice cream in record speed.

SHE WAS a puzzle. One Rick itched to figure out. He knew she was interested. They had chemistry, no doubt about it. So why the hesitation?

He looked at her profile as they walked along the moonlit beach. Two other couples strolled up ahead of them but no one else appeared to be around. He wondered what she'd do if he pulled her into his arms and urged her down onto the sand. Kissed her until neither of them could breathe. Slid his hand beneath the top of her sundress and touched her nipples.

Several times tonight they'd hardened and beaded against the silky pale yellow fabric. He'd had to look away, or embarrass himself. Every time he'd gotten too interested in any part of her anatomy, he'd silently recited baseball stats to cool down his body's reaction.

"Wanna go for a swim?" he asked, and she turned abruptly to look at him.

The moon was in the wrong spot for him to see her face clearly, but he could easily imagine the surprise in her beautiful green eyes. The way she wrinkled her cute upturned nose that used to be sprinkled with freckles.

"In the ocean? Now?"

"Yes on both counts."

She wrapped her arms around herself. "Are you crazy?"

"What are you talking about? You used to humiliate me into going swimming with you in Clear Lake after dark."

"A lake is different."

"Yeah, it's worse. All that vegetation growing on the bottom that used to wrap around our legs." The memory made him shudder.

She stopped and looked at him. "You were afraid?"

"Damn straight."

"You never told me."

"Yeah, right. Like I'd have admitted to a girl that I was too scared to follow her."

She laughed. "Yeah, I guess not."

He took both of her hands and pulled her toward him. "What are you afraid of, Carly?"

"Nothing." Her laugh was nervous and her breathing quick.

"Everyone is afraid of something."

She tried to twist out of his hold, but he wouldn't let her. "I'm *afraid* that if you don't let me go I'll have to hurt you."

"Cute. Now be serious."

She was close enough that with one small tug he could kiss her. He wanted to run his hands down her bare back, feel the silky soft skin under his palms. He'd dreamed about her last night, about them lying naked on a bed of autumn leaves.

Like most dreams it had been weird, the past getting confused with the present, adult images mixed with the carefree spirit of youth. He'd wakened feeling happy—happier than he'd felt in years. Odd how he hadn't thought much about her for the past twelve years, yet as soon as he'd seen her he'd felt the same connection they'd had as kids.

"Are you afraid that we'll start something we can't finish?" he asked, while urging her closer.

"No." She stiffened. "I don't know."

"Christ, Carly, I'm not asking you to marry me."

"Good." She yanked her hand away and started back toward the hotel.

"Come on." He caught up with her in three long strides. "Don't get huffy. I was trying to make a point."

With all the lights coming from the hotel, he could clearly see the annoyance on her face, the pink in her cheeks.

"I shouldn't have eaten that sundae," she murmured and kept walking. "I'm not feeling well."

"I'm not buying it." He'd lost the smile. "I thought we were getting along great."

She stopped but looked away from him, out toward the ocean.

"We are."

He took her hand again. "So what's the problem?"

"It's not you. Really."

"Hard to believe."

She sighed. "Being at this place—with Ginger behaving like she is—and then seeing you... It just feels awkward. I don't know..."

Rick let the thoughts gel in his head. She hadn't changed from the small-town girl he remembered. Still a little inhibited, worried that she should be the good girl and not embarrass her father the pastor.

"You're not in Oroville, Carly. No one here is going to pass judgment on you."

"It's not that." She made a sound of disgust. "This feels weird."

"Because you know me."

She nodded, looking pretty miserable. "I can't help it."

He wasn't sure how they could get past the whole history part. They'd swapped tall stories, confided a few secrets. In an odd way, he understood.

Maybe she was right. Not just about having history together being a bad thing, but because they'd already been intimate. The dangerous kind of intimacy. She knew some of his flaws. She'd unknowingly salved some of the pain he'd experienced by being an only and unwanted child.

"Hey," he said, nudging her the way he had when they were kids. "What if I promise to pretend I don't remember you if I ever go back to Oroville?"

She stared at him, surprise turning to what looked like panic. "You wouldn't ever go back to Oroville, would you?"

He shrugged. "You never know."

She took a step back. Maybe it was just the way the moonlight settled on her face, but she looked really pale. "I really don't feel well. No kidding," she said, and took off.

He didn't call her back and didn't follow her, either. He just stared after her, digesting what had just happened. Not that he knew for sure what had gone through that pretty head of hers. But she very clearly was spooked about something. Was she that afraid of tarnishing her good-girl image?

Even back when they were kids she was sometimes skittish about what her father's congregation saw or thought. But surely she'd outgrown that. Carly was too smart, too confident and had too much zest for life and for its little mysteries. God forbid that she'd ever forfeit a dare.

He smiled, thinking about old times, about how curiosity and enthusiasm had gotten her grounded for a few days. Even that hadn't stopped her. She'd sent notes in paper airplanes to him from her room. He'd hate to see her shut down, trying to fit in some perfect little mold that didn't suit her. Carly Saunders might live in a small town, but she was no small-town girl. And if he had to prove it to her, he would.

5

"THIS IS MY first time here. What about you?" Steve asked while shoving the sun-streaked hair off his forehead.

"My first time, too." Carly liked him already, even though she'd only met him ten minutes ago. He'd sat beside her at the bar while she waited for Ginger, but unlike some of the Neanderthals that she'd encountered earlier at the pool, he seemed well-mannered and even a little shy.

"What do you think of it?"

"The resort?"

He nodded, and then sipped his beer.

"To be perfectly honest, I'm not sure."

A slow grin spread across his face. "Me, too. A friend talked me into coming, but this isn't exactly my scene."

"It is rather overwhelming." She watched two women who seemed totally comfortable walking through the lobby wearing little more than a G-string.

His gaze followed hers and his eyes widened. He took a big gulp of beer. "That's putting it mildly."

Carly smiled. "Where are you from?"

"Hot Springs, Arkansas, and you sure don't see

women dressed like that in hotel lobbies there. What about you?"

"Utah."

"Where?"

"I guarantee you haven't heard of the town."

"You never know."

She hesitated, not wanting to give that much information. "Cedar City." She considered it a small fib, since Cedar City was only fifty miles away.

His eyebrows went up and the grin spread across his face again. "You win."

Relieved, she smiled. That was a valuable lesson. No more asking personal questions.

His gaze fell to her nearly finished strawberry daiquiri. "May I order you another one of those?"

"No, thanks. I'm meeting someone."

"Oh." The disappointment in his eyes made her realize her error.

Darn it. He might not have a lot of personality, but she was hoping he'd ask her to dinner so she could get to know him better. She made a show of looking around. "Yup, she said she'd be here by now. But she's always late."

The interest was back in his face. "Your roommate?"

She nodded. "Ginger."

He took another sip of beer, and then noisily cleared his throat. "Do you guys always eat dinner together?"

"Well, only if—"

"There you are. I've been looking all over for you."

Carly cringed when she heard Rick's voice. Why

did he have to show up now? Slowly she swiveled around in her seat. "Hi. What's up?"

"I'd hoped to catch you for lunch." He looked over her head and held up a hand. "Bartender, I'll have what the lady is having, and would you like another?" he asked her.

She slid a look at Steve who had turned to face the bar while he sipped his beer. "No, thanks, I don't want anything. I'm meeting Ginger."

"No, you aren't. She told me to tell you she's gone parasailing with Tony." He leaned close to her with familiarity.

She glared at him, her annoyance growing when she realized she'd actually responded by shifting toward him.

He turned to Steve. "Hi."

Steve mumbled an acknowledgment.

"Oh, I'm sorry," Carly quickly spoke up, leaning back, trying to put as much distance between her and Rick as possible. "Steve, this is my *old friend* Rick."

Rick laughed. "Right."

Steve stood abruptly and laid some beads on his tab. "Nice meeting you, Carly." He nodded at Rick. "You, too."

Carly started to ask him to wait. Ask him what he'd been about to say about dinner. She bit her lip. No way could she say something like that in front of Rick. Instead, she forced a smile. "Nice meeting you, too. Maybe I'll see you around."

She doubted Steve heard. He'd already headed for the elevators. She watched him disappear and then turned to Rick. "What are you doing?"

"What?" His look of exaggerated innocence made her want to throw something.

"You know darn well what you just did."

The bartender arrived with two daiquiris, and Rick used the distraction to his full advantage. When he was through making small talk with the guy about the ingredients of a new drink that was advertised, he turned back to Carly and smiled.

"What have you been doing all day?" he asked, leaning close as if he had the right.

"Rick..." She growled. "That was so unfair."

"What?"

"Steve was about to ask me to dinner."

"That guy?" He inclined his head.

"Yes, that guy. And his name is Steve."

Rick shook his head. "Nah, he's not right for you."

That startled a laugh out of her. "You just met him."

"True, but I could tell just by the way he tucked his tail between his legs and ran."

"You barged in. You made it look like we're having a thing."

"That shouldn't have scared him off. You told him we were friends." He shook his head. "Nope. You're a strong, intelligent woman. You need someone more your equal."

Surprised pride surged through her. He looked serious. That was his impression of her. "Look, Rick, it's not that I don't appreciate your being my guidance counselor." She slid off the barstool while she could still make an exit with dignity. "But butt out."

CARLY LAY on her stomach on the bed, watching Ginger pull one dress after another out of the closet. Amazing how she'd fitted that many clothes in two suitcases.

"How does this one look?" Ginger held up a lime-green, straight-cut sheath that ended at mid thigh.

"Great."

"That's what you said about the last one."

"Because they all look great. What else do you want me to say?"

Ginger sighed. "This is silly."

"Amen."

"No, I mean it's not like I'm going to have it on for that long."

Carly groaned and buried her face in the pillow. "I do not want to hear this."

"What did you say?" Ginger asked, already distracted by a violet-colored dress with spaghetti straps.

"Eventually you're going to wear them all so what does it matter which one you wear tonight?"

"Hmm." Ginger scrunched up her nose. "Good point." She took another look at the lime-green dress. "I think this is it. What about you? What are you wearing tonight?"

Carly rolled onto her back and stared at the ceiling. "I'm going to stay in tonight and order something from room service."

"You're kidding, right?" Ginger moved to the bed and loomed over her. "Carly Saunders, tell me you're kidding."

"I'm tired, okay?"

"No, it's not okay. We only have five more days

left here and—'' Ginger smiled. ''Ah, I get it. Rick is coming up to the room.''

''No.'' Carly sat up and met her friend's eyes meaningfully. ''And don't you dare tell him I'm here.''

Ginger sank to the edge of the bed. ''I don't understand you at all. He's a really nice guy. Funny, witty, smart...and aye Chihuahua...'' She fanned herself with her hand. ''What great buns.''

''I know. He is a great guy. But he's also somebody I could regret.''

Ginger frowned. ''You really like him, huh?''

''It's complicated.''

''So, think out loud. Maybe you'll find a solution.''

''There is only one wise thing to do. That's to stay away from Rick.''

''You know, you could 'regret' doing that, too.''

Carly shook her head. ''I really do like him, Ginger, but nothing can ever come of it. We want different things in life. That's why the anonymity thing would work so well. Just a good time. No heavy talking or soul-baring and then later worrying about what the other person thinks or expects.''

''And then, of course, there are your parents.''

''What do you mean?'' Carly frowned. Sometimes she got a little touchy about being a pastor's daughter. Her father was great. Kind. Understanding. Tolerant. People automatically assumed he was a strict disciplinarian who demanded she walk a straight line.

''They know Rick, right?''

''Yeah, sort of. Not well, but still...''

Ginger's expression turned sympathetic. ''I can see why you want to be cautious.''

A thought struck Carly. "Does it bother you at all that Rick is Tony's friend and I have a connection there?"

Without hesitation, Ginger shook her head. "It's not the same."

"Of course not." Carly smiled. "You'll have a great week, great memories and never see Tony again."

The stricken look on Ginger's face stopped Carly. It was fleeting, but very real. And then Ginger smiled. Not her usual smile, it was more forced. Enough to concern Carly.

"Ginger?"

"Good God, look at the time." She jumped up. "I have only half an hour to get ready. Would you help with my hair if it starts getting weird?"

"Of course."

Ginger stopped at the bathroom door. "And I suggest you get a move on, too. You're not staying in the room by yourself. Or I *will* tell Rick where you are."

ALL THROUGH her solitary dinner, Carly couldn't shake her concern for Ginger. She was asking for trouble if she thought Tony was looking for a committed relationship. Rick had already implied that Tony was a player. That was pretty obvious to Carly, and she hadn't see any harm since she'd known all Ginger wanted was a week of fun.

God, she hoped that hadn't changed. Heck, it had only been a couple of days. Everything was still exciting and new. Ginger would get over him.

Carly hoped.

She briefly closed her eyes. That's exactly what she didn't want to have happen between her and Rick. She didn't want to spend hours sitting in her old room in Oroville, wondering if he would call, yet hoping he wouldn't.

Her parents were wonderful, broad-minded people, and even though the rest of the town wasn't very good at minding their own business, it wasn't even about that. Her dilemma was about spending her life wanting something she couldn't have. She needed stability. Rick needed diversity and excitement.

He'd never consider living in Oroville. The mere thought boggled the mind. But even if he came to visit her...

She mentally shook herself. No need to go there. Nothing was going to happen between her and Rick, she'd decided. Period. She'd find some guy to hook up with for the rest of the week, and Rick would end up finding someone, too.

The bar where she'd agreed to meet Ginger and Tony was already packed. Couples spilled over from the dance floor, bumping chairs and tables and waitresses carrying trays of drinks.

Carly shrunk back closer to the bar. She shouldn't have come. Ginger and Tony had probably already forgotten and slipped away somewhere to do whatever.

She tried to concentrate on the Dire Straits lyrics the band played with amazing talent. Maybe she should at least have a drink....

"Would you like to dance?"

Carly looked up into a pair of light blue eyes. She'd

seen this guy before. At the pool. Or maybe in the lobby. He had a great smile and nice broad shoulders. She liked that he dressed so normally: new jeans and a long-sleeved white shirt rolled up to the middle of his forearms.

"Um, yeah, sure."

She let him lead her to the dance floor. The song had slowed and he put his hands on her waist.

"I better warn you. I'm not the best dancer," he said, his voice so low she could barely hear him above the noise.

"Good. I'm pretty bad myself."

He grinned. "I'm Bob."

"Carly."

He slid his hands to the small of her back and shuffled out of time with the music as he pulled her in closer. She looped her arms around his neck.

"You smell good," he whispered. "Is that jasmine?"

"You win the prize."

"Yeah?" He pulled back to smile down at her.

"Excuse me." Rick appeared, and he put a hand on Bob's shoulder. "May I cut in?"

Bob blinked. Clearly confused, he frowned at Rick and then at Carly. "Well, yeah, I guess."

"No." Carly kept her arms around Bob's neck even though he'd slackened his hold. "Ignore him," she told Bob and tried to steer him deeper into the crowd.

"Ah, honey, come on." Rick edged along with them. "Are you still mad?"

"Don't call me honey. Go away."

Bob tensed. "Would you like me to get rid of him?"

God, she was tempted. Sighing, she dropped her arms from around his neck. The last thing she wanted was to cause a scene. Or to let Rick get punched out.

"No, thanks." She stepped away. "Maybe we'll see each other later, huh?"

Bob didn't say anything, only frowned.

"Bob, the lady said—" Rick began.

But she grabbed him by his shirtsleeve and dragged him toward the door. Once they got outside, away from the noise, she turned to him and glared. "You're really ticking me off."

His eyebrows rose innocently again. "Why? I just wanted to dance with you."

She folded her arms across her chest. "I bet they have stalking laws even way out here."

"Give me a break. Tony and Ginger told me you were here. They had something else to do, so..." He gave a small bow. "I offered to show you a good time."

Carly clenched her teeth. Ginger was dead meat. "Maybe I should have let Bob clean your clock. That would have been a good time for me."

Rick grinned. "You wouldn't have done that. Especially since I rescued you."

She sighed. "Rescued?"

"Not a good choice."

"What?"

"Bob. Not right for you either."

"For goodness sake, we were only dancing."

"If you could call it that," he teased.

"It's none of your business anyway." She threw up her hands. "Forget it. Why do I bother?"

She started to walk away, but he captured her wrist and spun her back around to face him. He kissed her before she could utter a protest. She let her arms drop to her sides. She didn't resist, but she didn't exactly cooperate either.

He finally pulled back to look at her. With the back of his hand, he brushed the hair away from her face. "How did you get so beautiful?"

The light from the bar illuminated his face. He wasn't laughing or teasing. His eyes had darkened and he leaned down to kiss her again.

His lips were warm and gentle but insistent and, in spite of herself, she let him part hers with his tongue. She closed her eyes and breathed in the perfumed air. Flowering trees and shrubs surrounded them. The noise from the bar seemed to fade.

The moon was high and bright and gave just enough light to make the whole scene feel surreal. Except what was happening was real. And this was Rick. And tomorrow, in the cold light of day, she'd have to face him.

Breathless, she moved back, her knees shaky. "Why can't you just go away?" she whispered.

"Why?"

"I've already told you."

"What you did was give me mixed signals. You can't flip from hot to cold and not give me any reason."

"I'm sorry. You're right. I shouldn't have left anything open for speculation." She looked him in the eyes. "It won't work, Rick. It can't. Yes, it's probably my problem, but there it is."

He molded his palm to her waist, then down over her hip. "Are you sure?"

She nodded, she hoped with conviction. Not that she felt any resolve whatsoever with his hands doing magical things to her body. Her nipples had tightened and the urge to squeeze her thighs together was almost too great to ignore.

"Do you know how crazy it makes me to see you with all these guys I know you've only just met, yet you won't spend time with me?"

"All these guys? Please."

"Two in one day."

She laughed, trying not to think about how flattered she was. "They seemed very nice when I was talking to them."

"You know what they're after."

"And you're not?"

He lowered his hands. "That's different."

"Right."

"I know you. I like you. You wouldn't be just a conquest for me."

Her heart raced. "Why can't I be your friend?"

"You can."

She waited for him to say something else, but then realized he was done. "You said something about maybe visiting Oroville again. It'll be like old times. I'll show you our town's new additions. And I promise not to make you go swimming in the lake."

He didn't smile at her teasing. "It won't be like old times, Carly. You know that."

"It could be if we cool it."

"And what if I promise never to show my face in Oroville again?"

Carly sighed. "Don't make this out to sound sordid."

"I'm just trying to understand."

"You probably can't. So can we leave it alone?"

"How about a little harmless necking?" He nudged her chin up. "Would that count?"

She laughed, trying hard not to be mesmerized by his bedroom eyes. "I should have let Bob take care of you."

"Hey, he's got at least forty pounds on me. How would you sleep at night if he'd pulverized me?"

"Probably pretty well. I wouldn't have to worry about you popping up every moment."

"I'm hurt."

"Poor baby."

"Kiss me and make it better."

Her pulse picked up speed. As if she didn't know this was coming. "If I kiss you, will you go away?"

"Later." He smiled. "And only if you tell me again."

6

CARLY GAVE the pool area a good looking over before she ventured onto the deck and claimed a lounge chair. No Rick in sight. Thank goodness.

Earlier this morning he'd left a message asking her to go water skiing with him and Ginger and Tony and two others. She hadn't responded, and she hoped he'd taken off without her. So far, so good. After last night maybe he'd finally gotten the hint.

Sunbathers already took most of the lounge chairs, but she found one close to the shade of a palm tree and shook out her beach towel. At eleven the sun was already really hot and she didn't have much of a base on her fair skin. Her bare shoulders prickled with the heat and the clear blue pool water was looking better by the second.

She sat before she untied her sarong and then pulled it away from her body as she reclined. After wearing the new bikini for two days now, she still hadn't gotten used to its skimpy cut. Why had she let Ginger talk her into buying the darn thing? Bad enough it had been way too expensive, she'd never wear it again. Especially not in Oroville. The mere thought made her shudder.

"Mind if I take this chair?"

Shading her eyes, she looked up at a husky young man with a short military-style haircut.

"Of course not. Go ahead."

"Thanks." He had a baby face and a friendly dimpled smile that made it hard to guess his age. He looked barely twenty-one.

She expected him to drag the chair away but he laid a towel over it and then stretched out. He'd brought a Stephen King novel with a bookmark tucked in halfway through the book. He didn't open it right away but stared out over the pool.

He was going to start talking to her. She just knew it. Not that she was necessarily interested but... Immediately she looked around. More people were entering the area. Only a few vacant chairs remained. Still no Rick.

She started to breathe easier, relaxing back so that her face got full sun. She'd applied a sufficient amount of sun block so she wasn't worried. Under the protection of her sunglasses, she glanced over at the man nearby. He still hadn't picked up the book but seemed preoccupied with watching the people splash around in the pool.

She wiggled into a comfortable position half expecting she'd fall asleep. God knew she hadn't gotten enough rest last night. Not after Rick had insisted on walking her to her room. She'd let him go with her as far as the elevators, not sure who she trusted less, Rick or herself.

It was getting more and more difficult to say no to him. Just being near him clouded her ability to reason. She wanted to throw up her hands and say "take me."

But she knew herself too well. She'd think about him. For weeks. Maybe even for months, long after she was ensconced in her teaching job and Rick was halfway across the world, having forgotten all about her.

She'd think about him because he brought out that small wild part of her that wanted to say the hell with it all. The part of her that told her she had only one life to live, so why should she live it to please others? But the truth was, she'd made the choice to return. She wanted to live in Oroville. It was familiar. It was home.

She had only four days left. She could be strong. Resist him. Ignore the way his voice got low and sexy when he whispered in her ear. Or the way he trailed light kisses up the side of her neck. The way his smile melted her insides and made wet heat pool between her thighs.

"Excuse me, ma'am?"

She opened her eyes and brought her head up.

"Are you okay?" It was the guy next to her, the concern in his eyes making him look older.

"Yes, I'm fine."

He looked embarrassed. "You were moaning. You probably dozed and had a bad dream."

"Probably," she muttered, a lot more embarrassed than he was. "Thanks."

"Look, the cocktail waitress is making her rounds." He inclined his head toward a short blonde in a red bikini carrying a tray. "Can I buy you a drink?"

"A bottle of water would be nice."

He grinned and signaled for the woman. "I came

here with a couple of buddies, but I sure haven't seen much of them.''

"I know what you mean. I haven't seen much of the friend I came with either.''

"Yeah.'' He shrugged. "I didn't know it was going to be this kind of place.''

She didn't have to ask what he meant. All around guests had paired off into couples, even those who'd walked in alone not fifteen minutes ago. "So, are you on leave?''

He made a face, his hand automatically going to his short-cropped hair. "It shows that much, huh?''

"Actually, I shouldn't have assumed you were in the military.''

"That's okay. I'm an air force sergeant.''

"A sergeant?''

He gave her a wry smile. "Don't say it. I know, I look too young.''

She shrugged apologetically. "You really do.''

"I'm twenty-five.''

She sighed. He was her age. "I'm Carly, by the way.''

"Dan,'' he responded. "Daniel Peterson.''

Carly just smiled. He didn't need to know her last name. Not that she thought anything would come of this conversation. But if it did… "What do you do for the air force?''

"I'm with the Air Commandos stationed in Florida.''

"Is that some sort of special ops?''

He nodded. "We work with Navy Seals, Green Berets, that sort of thing.''

She smiled. "Sounds very elite."

The cocktail waitress showed up to take their orders. She already carried bottled water on her tray and gave one to Carly, and then wrote down the spicy tomato juice Dan ordered.

He emphasized that he wanted only juice and no alcohol which didn't surprise Carly. He had a terrific, well-attended body. Heavy duty working out obviously wasn't foreign to him. Which probably meant he was careful about what he consumed. Maybe his job required top physical condition.

No matter the reason, it was darn intimidating. She glanced at her thighs. They used to be so firm in her soccer days. Now they seemed to show every doughnut and Milky Way she ate.

"So what do you do, Carly?" he asked once the waitress had move on.

"I'm a teacher. Or I will be in a couple of months. I just finished graduate school."

They made small talk for the next ten minutes and she found she really liked him. He was interesting and funny, and seemed genuinely interested in what she had to say.

When he suggested they go for a dip in the pool, it didn't occur to her to say no—until she stood. And then she wished like crazy she was wearing her old one-piece suit.

Her thoughts dominoed and she started thinking about Rick again, which reminded her to check out the area. He had a knack for showing up as soon as she started talking to someone of the opposite sex.

To her relief, there was still no sign of him. He was

probably in the middle of the Caribbean on a speedboat, and if she was smart she'd take advantage of the opportunity to circulate.

When Dan offered her a hand as she stepped down into the pool, she accepted his help with a flirtatious smile. He kept hold of her hand a moment too long but she didn't mind. Though he wasn't really her type, he was nice and gentlemanly and...

Water splashed in her face and she reared back.

"What the hell?" Dan got a faceful, too.

Someone had dived in foolishly close. When he or she surfaced, Carly was going to...

Rick.

He popped up, shaking his head and spraying water everywhere. "Hey," he said, grinning. "I didn't expect to see you here."

She opened her mouth but nothing came out. He was just too much.

"What the hell are you doing?" The veins in Dan's thick neck popped out. He glared ominously at Rick.

"Sorry, buddy." Rick offered him an apologetic hand. "I wanted to say hi to my friend here."

"I'm not your buddy."

"No, I guess not." Rick glanced wryly at her.

Carly hid a smile. He deserved this dressing down.

"Hey." Dan jabbed him hard in the chest. "You sure you wanna be a wise guy?"

"Feel free to jump in here anytime," Rick said to Carly.

She hesitated, but then decided Dan looked too angry. She put a hand out to get his attention when he suddenly grabbed Rick's arm and twisted it around his back.

Rick muttered a curse. "Come on. This is unnecessary."

"Please, Dan. He's a friend of mine. I know he didn't mean anything."

Rick tried to pull away but he couldn't. "I think you broke my friggin' hand."

She gasped. "Dan."

He glanced at her, hesitated, and then finally let Rick go, but shoved him backward.

"Thank you," she murmured, and then gave Rick a pointed look.

"Hey, pal." Dan got Rick's attention and then landed a fist in his face. "Now we're even."

Rick stumbled back but didn't go down.

Carly stifled a scream. People all around were staring. "You're crazy," she snapped at Dan.

He raised his eyebrows. "What?"

She went to Rick and put an arm around him. "Are you okay?"

"I'm going to kill the bastard."

"No, you aren't." Carly looked over her shoulder, hoping Dan hadn't heard that remark. Thankfully he was already heading out of the pool. "Come on, we're getting out of here."

"But that guy had no—"

"Shut up!" She led him to the other end and kept a firm hold of his elbow as they navigated the steps and got on the deck.

Several people stared as she forced him toward the pool bar. Darn, she wished she had her sarong but she didn't dare leave Rick unattended, nor did she want to get near Dan. She was liable to haul off and punch *him* in the face.

And here she'd thought he was such a nice guy. What a barbarian.

"Hey, we're passing the bar," Rick said as she steered him onto the path to the hotel.

"That's right."

"I could really use a cold beer about now."

"Great. Have a drink and next thing you know you'll be back in Dan's face saying something stupid."

"I don't want the beer. I want the can to hold against my eye."

She looked over at him. The side of his face was red, and she had no doubt he'd end up with some black-and-blue markings. "Does it hurt?"

"What do you think?"

"No need to get sarcastic. After all, it was your fault. What about your hand?"

"So I splashed some water. You think that was reason enough for him to hit me?"

"Of course not. You said he broke your hand." She squinted at it but it didn't look swollen.

"Nah, I think maybe my wrist is sprained. That's all." He grimaced when he flexed his hand. "My thumb might be out of joint."

"Come on." She let go of his arm, expecting him to follow. When he didn't, she stopped and turned around. He was looking at her bottom.

"Screw the sarong. You look terrific."

She wanted to smack him in the other eye. "Look, do you want to get some ice on that, or not?

"Yes, ma'am."

She waited for him to catch up, not wanting to give him any more chance to view her backside. Oh, God, how was she going to make it through the lobby in dental floss? It didn't matter that everyone else was dressed similarly. They obviously didn't feel self-conscious.

He slowed down. "Where are we going?"

She slid him an impatient glance and noticed his eye was starting to swell. "To the lobby bar to get ice."

"Why don't we just go to my room?"

She eyed him with suspicion. Although the thought of avoiding the lobby did appeal to her. An outside path could reach the elevators to his wing. And then another thought occurred to her. What the devil was she doing? Typically, she'd gone into rescue mode.

"You don't need me," she said. "You can go up to your room and get ice out of the machine."

He looked at her with hurt and disappointment in his eyes.

"Come with me."

"I need to go change."

"Why? Nobody but us will be in the room."

Right. No problem. "The longer you stand here arguing, the worse your eye is getting." Which was the truth. She wouldn't be surprised if it swelled shut soon.

"Who's arguing?"

"You don't need my help, Rick."

"I do. My hand is killing me. It'll be hard to get ice and I may even need to rig my thumb with a splint."

She hesitated, though he looked serious enough. "Okay, but just for a minute. Then I'm out of there."

He held his hands up in mock surrender. "Your call."

"Do you have your key?" she asked, sadly realizing that hers was pinned to her sarong. Fortunately that was all she'd left behind and the chances were good they'd still be there later.

"Yeah." He slid two fingers beneath the elastic waistband of his swim trunks and winced. "Damn."

":What?"

"I can't get to it."

"Where is it?"

"In a small inside pocket. You try."

She gave a startled laugh at the thought of reaching into his trunks.

He looked at her, an earnest, helpless expression on his face. "It's right near the waistband, a small cloth pocket."

"So why can't you reach it?"

"Because my thumb hurts like hell. Rambo really did a number on it." He gingerly touched the base. "Who was that guy, anyway?"

"I don't know. I'd just met him."

"What is he, a marine?"

"Air force. He said he was an Air Commando or something."

"Great. One of those. Guess I should just be grateful he didn't kill me."

She rolled her eyes. "All right, where is this pocket?"

"Right here." He indicated an area above his right hip.

She glanced around. No one else was on the path behind them. Ahead people milled around outside the open lobby but no one paid attention. Besides, it wasn't as if she were going to stick her hand down his trunks.

She tentatively pinched the elastic waistband between her thumb and forefinger.

"It's more to the right. But if you want to find it by Braille, I have no problem with— Ouch! What did you do that for?"

She'd barely snapped the elastic. "Knock it off or you're on your own."

"Not another peep out of me."

She stuck the tip of her fingers in and immediately found the pocket. Delving down a little farther, she located the key. She felt something else, like a piece of foil stuck to the key, and she brought them both out.

"I'll take that." Rick yanked it out of her hand before she got a look at it.

Of course it was none of her business. She slid a look at his hand, but he'd fisted whatever it was tightly. With his injured hand he held the key.

They continued to the elevator in silence. Stayed that way up to the tenth floor. When they got to his room, he pushed the key into the lock and then hesitated. "Sure hope the maid's been here."

He opened the door and groaned.

What a mess. Clothes were strewn about. Empty beer bottles sat on the desk. Bath towels were piled up outside the bathroom door.

Rick pushed the door wider for her. "Tony is a great friend. But I've never met a bigger slob."

"Another reason he and Ginger should get along well." Carly grinned. "Don't worry about it. Our room is just as bad. Ginger can never decide on what to wear and the girl doesn't understand the concept of a hanger."

He returned the smile, and then got serious. "Ginger knows this week is just—never mind."

"What were you going to say?"

"Tony's not the kind of guy who—". He paused, shaking his head. "Shouldn't have brought it up. None of my business." He headed straight for the ice bucket.

"She knows."

He caught Carly's gaze and held it. "You two had this week all figured out, huh?"

"What's that supposed to mean?"

His faint smile looked slightly sad. "I think it's finally sinking in how much I ruined your vacation."

"You didn't." She sighed, shrugging. "I'm still having a good time."

"Liar."

"Okay, you ruined my vacation. Happy? Now give me the ice bucket. I'll get the ice."

He passed it to her, his eye really starting to look nasty. "Down the corridor to the left."

"I'll have to make a compress. Lie down while I get the ice."

"Hmm, what did you have in mind?" He waggled his eyebrows up and down, and then grimaced. "Ouch."

She shook her head. He was incorrigible.

He slid her a suggestive look. "Come here."

"What?" Her skin started to tingle. Her nipples tightened. One look and she was a marshmallow. Toasted. All soft and squishy inside with absolutely no restraint.

He reached for her hand and pulled her close. "Have I told you how great you look in that bikini?"

She swallowed. "This is so not what I had in mind."

"No?" He kissed the side of her mouth, the line of her jaw.

Even as Carly shook her head, she lifted her chin to give him better access to her throat. He didn't stop there but nibbled and licked his way to her collarbone. His tongue dipped down into the cleft between her breasts.

She stumbled backward, bringing the ice bucket up to her chest, clutching it tightly. She was crazy. He didn't really need her help. He wasn't that hurt. Nor did she feel any responsibility for what had happened. That's not why she'd agreed to stay.

She was crazy, that's why. Certifiably insane. It was like knowing fire burned but wanting to touch it anyway. And she would get burned. She knew that way down deep where her intuition never failed her. Being with Rick was dangerous. No, not just dangerous. When they were kids, together they'd been dangerous, but now they were explosive, like dynamite just inches from a flame.

She had to get out of here before she dove under the covers with him and didn't come up for the rest of the week. And then where would she be? Back in Oroville, pining away for months, maybe years. But she had willpower. Just four more days.

No problem.

Yeah, right.

7

RICK KICKED Tony's clothes into the closet and then swept his empty beer bottles into a wastebasket. He really liked the guy. He considered him his best friend, but this kind of inconsiderate stuff really pissed Rick off.

They'd made a deal dividing up custody of the room. So far, Rick hadn't needed the privacy. But damn it, it could happen. He could get lucky. If only Carly would relax.

He knew for certain why she was here. What he didn't understand was why she'd changed her mind. It wasn't personal, he knew. They had chemistry. Loads of it. Maybe that's what scared her.

Though it didn't scare him. They both had jobs to go back to in different states. Careers that were important to them. They could keep in touch, maybe even meet for a weekend in Las Vegas now and then. Who knew where it could all lead? Maybe they'd find they were soulmates.

He used a damp face towel to wipe off the sticky beer residue from the table. His thumb really wasn't bad. By this evening, his eye would be another matter. For that, he did want ice.

He glanced at the bedside clock. She'd been gone

nearly five minutes. He hoped she hadn't decided to take off. That wouldn't surprise him. She'd obviously been trying to avoid him. He should have accepted that the first time he realized she'd dodged him. There was a countless number of good-looking women on the prowl. Bold women who knew what they wanted and weren't afraid to express themselves.

He'd passed up several opportunities he'd later probably hate himself for missing. But Carly was never far from his thoughts. His memory of their two summers was constantly being jogged. They'd had some great times, just the two of them. Exploring the woods and streams and beaver dams.

Whenever he couldn't do something as well as she, Carly had never belittled him. She'd shrugged and said she had more practice. Pointed out that he'd done so many things she hadn't. As much as he loved his grandmother, even she'd had a habit of comparing Rick to his father, who'd always been at the top of his class, the head of his field.

How could a son compete? He couldn't. But that hadn't stopped Rick from trying. Look where it had gotten him. Trapped in a job he hated. Venting his frustration, he wadded up one of Tony's discarded shirts and slammed it into the closet.

Even during their short acquaintance as kids, Carly had been someone to admire. Not that he'd appreciated the fact at the time. Brave, inquisitive, outspoken, always so damn sure of herself. Even back then she knew she wanted to be a teacher. Lectured anyone who would listen on what an important field teaching was.

He'd thought she was nuts. Who wanted to be stuck in a classroom when the whole world was an adventure, full of possibilities and excitement? He still couldn't understand her enthusiasm, but he admired her conviction.

He glanced at the clock again and muttered a curse. She was gone, or she'd have returned by now. Expecting to find the ice bucket sitting outside the door, he opened it.

Carly stood there, just staring, the bucket filled with ice in her hands. She blinked at him. "Hi."

He smiled. "Forgot the key?"

She nodded, her cheeks pinking a little, probably because she'd been thinking about making a break for the elevators.

"I thought maybe you'd had second thoughts." He opened the door wider and she walked in. He couldn't take his eyes off her backside. So round and firm-looking. His body reacted immediately.

"About what?"

"Being here with me."

She laughed. "Second thoughts? More like fifth and sixth."

"I'll try not to take offense."

"I'd rather you try to keep your hands to yourself."

"You sure?" He smiled at the dirty look she gave him and then paused at the decorative mirror over the table to check out his eye. He winced at the puffy redness, and almost headed back out the door to go smash Rambo in the face. Man, by tomorrow he was going to have one hell of a shiner.

"At least it isn't swollen shut." Carly made a place

on the cluttered desk for the ice bucket. Her back was to him, her rounded derriere making his pulse race, and he had to look away.

She turned around, but that didn't help. Her bikini top was barely up to its task. Her full breasts mounded over the top and her nipples strained against the fabric.

"You have any clean facecloths?" she asked.

"I'll go see." He beat it into the bathroom and splashed his face with cold water before grabbing two washcloths off the rack. "I found a couple."

"Perfect." She shook out one damp hand, and then dragged her palm down her thigh. She stared down at her bare leg as if she'd forgotten she wore next to nothing.

"Um, would you have a T-shirt or something I could borrow?" she asked, after accepting the face-cloths. "Or a robe. A robe would be good."

A robe? He wasn't that chivalrous. He liked the view too much. It took only seconds to find a clean aloha shirt. "How about this?"

She eyed the silky blue-and-cream floral shirt with misgivings. "It's short."

"It's a shirt," he said dryly.

She sighed and snatched the shirt, muttering thanks while she slipped into it. After fastening every button, she wrapped one of the facecloths around a chunk of ice cubes that had melted together.

Rick sat back and congratulated himself on not making a total ass out of himself. He still managed to get a great view of her legs and when she turned just so, he glimpsed the curves of her backside cheeks.

"I think this will work," she said, studying her

handiwork. "This plastic bag was in the bucket. I put it around the facecloth so it won't drip."

"Good idea." His voice cracked and he cleared his throat.

She frowned briefly and then asked. "Would you be more comfortable lying down or sitting up?"

"I don't know. What about you?"

"Rick." She put a hand on her hip. The shirt rode up just enough for him to get a good look at the juncture of her inner thighs.

"Okay. Point taken." He abruptly turned around, pulled out a chair from the desk and sank into it.

She frowned thoughtfully as she handed him the wrapped ice. "You know it probably would be better if you lay down, or else you're liable to end up with one heck of a stiff neck."

He slouched down, rested his head back, and tried to balance the cold pack on his eye. She was right. It was too awkward. He'd have to continually hold it in place.

She went to Tony's bed and plumped up the pillows.

"Nope. Wrong one." He pointed to the queen closer to the bathroom. "That one's mine. Besides, you don't have to do that."

"I know." She went to his bed and did the same thing, then doubled up the pillows before resting them against the headboard. "There. That should do it. If the pillows are too high, you can use one to rest your elbow while you hold the ice pack."

He smiled, thinking about something that had happened the last summer they'd spent together.

The corners of her mouth lifted. "What?"

"I was just thinking again about when you creamed me with the butt of that fishing pole."

"And you're smiling? You weren't too happy with me, as I recall."

He automatically fingered the scar the accident had left on the side of his chin. "I was thinking about how you immediately took over, applying pressure to stop the bleeding. And here you were just a kid. You were awesome."

She pointed to the bed. "Are you going to wait until this ice melts?"

"No, ma'am." He got up and bounced onto the bed, letting out a yowl when he accidentally bumped his thumb. "Damn it all to hell."

She shook her head, and then gently placed the ice pack on his eye. He went to hold it in place and captured her hand. Her gaze shot to his. He saw the way her throat worked as she swallowed hard. "Anything else before I go?"

"Stay."

She withdrew her hand and he reluctantly released it. "I'm missing the best part of the sun."

"The worst part. You don't want to burn." He trailed a finger down the front of her thigh. "Your skin is so soft. Don't let the sun ruin it."

She moistened her lips and moved back just out of his reach. "How's the thumb?"

"Better. I think it's just sprained."

"Well, that's bad enough."

"I've had worse."

Her lips curved into a teasing smile. "Do you make a habit of getting into fights?"

He grunted. "That wasn't a fight. He sucker-punched me. If I had wanted to—"

"Okay, okay, let's skip the macho baloney," she said, still smiling. "Don't ruin my opinion of you now."

"How?"

"I liked that you didn't have to fight back. That you could just walk away instead of make things worse."

He shrugged one shoulder. "I've gotta admit. I wasn't always that level-headed."

"I know." She grinned again. "Remember when Wendell Jenkins purposely splashed me with a mud puddle? You chased him for three blocks."

"Oh, yeah. And you were right behind me."

"That little pip-squeak had been annoying me for half my life. Just because I always beat his butt at softball." She chuckled. "He struck out every time I pitched."

"Tell me about it. You used to whip my ass, too."

Carly grinned. She'd been more athletic than he was at the beginning, but his competitive nature had turned that around quickly. "Only when you were being so darn full of yourself. What?" she asked when he stared back with an odd expression on his face.

"You never swear."

"So?"

"Not even a *damn* or *hell* rolls off those pretty lips."

"I'd like to think I have a better vocabulary than that." Defensiveness sprung inside her like a geyser.

Just because she was the pastor's daughter people expected certain behavior out of her. Well, she was still her own person.

"I'm not criticizing you. I like it." He made a helpless gesture with his hand. "Obviously I swear sometimes, and I have no problem with anyone else doing it, but I don't know…" He looked a little sheepish. "I just like it that you don't swear."

She smiled, extremely pleased. "I won't mention anything about double standards."

"I never pretended to be politically correct."

"That's for sure."

"Jeez, talk about kicking a guy while he's down."

Laughing, she gestured to the door. "If I'm bothering you, I could leave—"

"Don't make me get up."

"And?"

His left eyebrow went up. "Dare me?"

At the old childhood taunt, giddiness rose in her chest. A vivid memory of the day he'd dared her to go skinny-dipping in Clear Lake flashed in her mind. "I dare you."

He removed the ice pack from his eye, revealing a mischievous gleam.

"Put that back on right now before the swelling gets worse. I was only kidding."

"Too late."

"Rick." She tried to sound stern, but excitement robbed her of breath.

"Remember that day at Clear Lake?" He swung his legs to the floor.

Slowly, she nodded, a little disconcerted that he seemed to have read her mind.

"I dared you to go skinny-dipping."

"I remember," she said, the memory not altogether pleasant.

She'd started to strip and he'd backed out. She'd been mortified. And hurt, although not until later as she'd lain in bed that night, wondering if he'd ever regard her as more than a buddy.

"You pulled off your jeans." He sat on the edge of the bed, his gaze wandering down her bare thighs.

"And you ran like a scared rabbit."

He laughed, his eyes abruptly coming up to meet hers. "Scared? More like terrified."

That, she hadn't expected. "Why?"

"Because I let the wrong head do my thinking."

She blinked. "Ah."

He grinned. "You were so young and I was at that dangerously stupid age when even popcorn made me think of sex."

"Popcorn?"

He nodded. "Bubble gum, toothpaste, you name it."

She laughed. "Yeah, I understand."

"You do?"

"What? You don't think girls think about sex, too?"

"Well, sure, but..." He stared solemnly at her. "What were you thinking that day?"

Carly considered her answer for a moment, wondering how truthful she wanted to be. "My initial reaction had been about the dare," she said slowly. "But then later that night, after you'd run off and left me at the lake, I started to—'' She shrugged. ''Why are we talking about this? It happened a million years ago.''

''Not quite that long.'' His smile was gentle. ''You started to what?''

''It's stupid.''

''Most things are at that age. Come on. Tell me.''

She shrugged, stalling.

Someone knocked at the door. Once. Twice. ''Housekeeping.''

Rick muttered a curse. ''You did that on purpose.''

Carly chuckled on her way to the door. ''Yeah, right. I used my psychic powers to make her come here.''

''Wait,'' he said, as she was about to open the door. ''Tell her to skip service today.''

She glanced around at the mess. ''I don't think so.''

He followed her gaze. ''Good point.''

''You can stay in bed with the ice pack. She can work around you. Or at least get the bathroom cleaned.''

''Or we could go out on the balcony while she's here. There are a couple of chairs out there.''

Carly heard the key in the lock and opened the door. Startled, the maid muttered something in Spanish and then giggled.

''Come on in.'' Carly opened the door wider, and smiled as the woman's eyes rounded on Rick, bare-chested, sitting on the bed, his swim trunks hidden by the tangle of sheets.

He stood, and the woman looked as if she were about to turn and run until she saw his trunks. Her round face split into a grin and she bent to stick a wedge under the door to keep it open.

Rick grabbed a couple of pillows off the bed and led the way outside to the balcony. Carly picked up the ice bucket to make sure the maid didn't dump it.

From the balcony, they had a partial view of the ocean and the sun hit them at an angle so that it was pleasantly warm rather than blistering hot. Rick dropped a pillow on one of the lounge chairs and then drew the other one closer.

Carly didn't object. It wasn't as if they could do anything out here. The closeness made it easier to talk. Although she wasn't sure how much of that she wanted to do.

"Hey, the icepack." She motioned with her chin. "It's not doing any good in your hand."

"Yes, ma'am." He plopped down, got his pillow just so and then placed the icepack on his eye.

Carly put the bucket at the foot of the other lounge chair. Then, gripping the railing, she leaned forward to feel the warm breeze on her face. "I can see why you love it here," she said. "The fragrant air, water so clean it sparkles. And I've never seen such snow-white sand. Truly a paradise."

When he didn't respond, she turned to look at him half expecting that he might have dozed off. He hadn't. He stared back at her, a faint smile on his lips.

For a moment he looked like the old Rick, the young boy full of enthusiasm and plans, and her heart squeezed. She quickly looked back out toward the ocean. Something had happened since then, something that had robbed him of the passion he'd once had for his career.

She wanted to ask, and since they were friends, it wouldn't be out of line. But that sort of discussion would breed intimacy. Something she couldn't afford. It was difficult enough not to give in, stretch out beside him and run her hands over his lean hard body. Have him cup her breasts and suckle them. Find the heat between her thighs.

Her nipples tightened at the thought, and she swallowed hard. Why the heck was she doing this to herself? An hour or two of passion was not worth months of worry or regret.

"You grip that railing any tighter and you'll have a sprained hand, too."

Carly looked over at him. He peered at her with curiosity. She loosened her hold and shrugged. "This is pretty high up. I like the scenery but looking down gives me the willies."

He took the icepack away from his eye and patted the lounge chair beside him. "Come sit here by me. You'll still get a great view."

She moved away from the railing and adjusted the hem of his shirt. Not that it covered much, but tugging at it made her feel marginally better. She stretched out on the chair and tried to relax her shoulders.

"Lean forward."

She frowned at him and realized he wanted to put the pillow behind her. She took it from him, and gave the icepack a meaningful look.

"All right already," he said, and ministered to his

eye. "Better be careful or I'm going to start thinking you actually like me."

"Don't be silly. Of course I like you."

"You deny you've been avoiding me?"

"No."

He let out a startled laugh. "Okay. That was honest. Even though you've wounded me."

She sighed. "I probably—" She laid her head back and closed her eyes. "I probably like you too much."

He was quiet for so long she was tempted to look at him. Finally, he asked, "What's wrong with that?"

She thought for a moment, wondering if she should bring up the subject. Heck, nothing ventured, nothing gained. "What do you see in our future?"

He shot her a wary look.

"A card or a call at Christmas? A postcard now and then? Or maybe no contact at all?"

"Or meet a couple of weekends a year in Vegas?"

"I'm serious, Rick."

"Shit." He lay back and stared at the blue sky.

"You are, too," she said only half aloud.

"I don't know. I haven't really thought about it." He grunted. "What's wrong with a weekend or two in Vegas? It's about midpoint between Oroville and L.A."

"Good grief. It's not about distance."

"Well, what is it about then?" He abruptly met her gaze. "Tell me you didn't come here to get banged."

She winced at his crudeness.

He settled back down and muttered, "Sorry, that was crass."

She seethed inside, mostly because it was the truth, and said aloud, it sounded awful.

"Look, I don't know what's going to happen. Maybe we'll leave here and find out we can't live without each other."

Carly swallowed, and turned her face toward the ocean. She didn't want her expression to give away any emotion. Not that she even knew what she was feeling. Numb. Scared. No, petrified was more like it. He couldn't mean that. He'd said it because that's what he thought she wanted to hear.

He sighed wearily. "I honestly don't know, Carly. Can't we just take things as they come?"

She stubbornly refused to look his way. She was right in not giving in. Her heart was too fragile when it came to Rick. He had the power to hurt her. If she let him.

Besides, she wasn't about to spend her life having a closet affair. She wanted a home and family of her own, a swing set in the backyard, holiday feasts with all the tradition and trimmings...

She stared mindlessly at the horizon. Sure, there was a lot to see in the world. But she was content to live in Oroville. And she didn't want anything upsetting the balance.

Rick hadn't said a word and she couldn't help but wonder what he was thinking. Reluctantly, she turned to him. He was asleep. Or so it seemed. His eyes were closed, the ice pack had slipped to his cheek and his lips were slightly parted.

Gee, good thing worrying didn't keep him awake.

She lay her head back and closed her eyes, letting the warm breeze soothe her jagged nerves. So quiet…so peaceful…

"CARLY, wake up."

She blinked a couple of times and tried to focus on Rick's face. He sat on the edge of her lounge chair, one hand cupping her cheek.

"Carly, come on, you gotta wake up. We have a problem."

"I wasn't asleep," she murmured and yawned at the same time.

"Right. Promise not to panic."

She bolted upright. "What's wrong?"

"Keep your voice down."

The sun had already set, she realized with a start, and adding darkness to the dimly lit sky was a cluster of rain clouds. Out of the corner of her eye, she saw that a lamp was on inside the room. She twisted around to see.

"Wait." Taking her by the shoulders, Rick stopped her. "I wouldn't if I were you."

"What are you talking about?"

His gaze stayed on her as he made a motion with his head toward the room. "We have company. And they're naked."

8

CARLY TURNED and stared in horror at Ginger and Tony in one of the queen beds. Abruptly she looked away. She hadn't really seen anything. Thanks to the sheets bunched up around them, she could only see Ginger's bare back and Tony's arm.

"When did they get here? Did they see you?" she asked Rick. "Did you knock?"

"I just woke up myself. They were kind of busy already."

"This is unbelievable." She started to turn around again and caught herself. "Shall we knock, let them know we're out here?"

"Be my guest."

"Why me?"

"It's your idea."

"It's your room."

He gave her a dry look. "Yeah, that makes sense."

"Then what should we do?"

"Wait."

She shook her head. "Why? It's going to be embarrassing no matter what we do. Waiting won't help."

"Not if we wait until they leave. They'd never know we were out here."

"That could take hours."

Rick laughed. "You give Tony way too much credit."

She had to stop and think for a moment, and then she chuckled. "Does it look as if they're close to finishing?"

He tugged on the hem of her shirt, and gave her a crooked smile. "How am I supposed to know?"

"I didn't mean it like that." God, she was thirsty. And warm. Probably because he was sitting so darn close, his thigh brushing hers, his musky male scent crowding her, making her a little light-headed. She glanced at the ice bucket, wondering if there were any ice cubes left. "Does it look as if they were getting their clothes?"

"Sex isn't a spectator sport."

"Huh?"

"I haven't been watching them."

Annoyed at the way he twisted her meaning, she let out a sound of disgust. He quickly cupped his hand over her mouth. The unnerving urge returned to draw his thumb between her lips. She reared back.

"Keep it down or we won't have to worry about how to get out of this."

Before she could respond, loud moans came from the room—first Ginger, and then Tony.

Carly sighed. "Let's just knock and get it over with. "I'll do it."

Rick grabbed her arm when she started to swing her legs to the other side. "I'd definitely wait. Sounds to me like they're close."

A giggle bubbled out before she could stop it. She cleared her throat.

Rick's lips lifted in a wide grin. "I'd feel better if Tony hadn't sworn he wasn't going to use our room this time. It was my turn."

Carly stared. "Excuse me?"

"No, not with you." He groaned. "Not with anyone. I mean, I just wanted to know I could come back to my own room to read or nap or do whatever."

She didn't say anything. None of her business.

"Hell, Carly, I haven't been with anyone else here."

She shrugged nonchalantly despite that her heart had done a somersault. "That's none of my concern."

"Obviously," he muttered, pushing a frustrated hand through his hair. "Let's play Ghost. That'll eat up some time."

"What's Ghost?"

"A word game." He lifted a brow. "You sure you haven't played it? You planning on sandbagging me?"

"No, I swear. I've never heard of it."

"Okay. It goes like this: the person who starts gives a letter, then the next person adds one and then it goes back to the first person and so forth until a word is made. It has to be at least a four-letter word and whoever gives the last letter loses."

"Where does the word *ghost* come in?"

"Every time you lose you get a letter from the word, and whoever ends up spelling *ghost* first loses."

She frowned. "Sounds complicated."

"It's not. Let's do a practice round."

"Go ahead. You first." She was too distracted by

what was going on inside, by the way his leg casually brushed hers, by the way his warm breath floated over her skin. She couldn't very well tell him to move. They had to keep their voices low as it was.

"Okay, let's see…" He looked off toward the ocean as he thought, his strong square chin jutting slightly. His lashes were thick and long. She hadn't really noticed before. Probably because his eyes always had her so mesmerized with their flecks of gold and green and passion.

"All right." He smiled at her, and her silly heart fluttered. *"L."*

"Now I give a letter, right?"

He nodded.

"Should I have a word in mind already or just shoot a letter out there?"

His brows dipped in a frown. "You aren't into this, are you?"

"I'm just a little distracted." She ignored his knowing smile. "Okay, you started with *L.* I'll add *I.*"

"Hmm. *L-I-C.*"

She grunted. One more letter and it would make a word. And not just any word. Darn it. She'd cornered herself.

"By the way," he said, "you can always call the other person on a word you don't think is possible."

She sighed. "All right, I get it."

"Call a letter."

"What's the point? I'll be out."

"Not necessarily."

"Lick is all I can think of."

He laughed softly. "I do like the way you think.

However, you could have said, for instance, *O* and hopefully gone on to spell *licorice.*"

Heat immediately invaded her cheeks. "I don't think I like this game."

"Give it a chance. You want to start?"

"No."

"Okay, *C.*" He shifted his weight, making the lounger rock. Casually he laid a hand on her arm for balance. "And don't forget, if the fourth letter forms a word, the game stops no matter which word you had in mind."

She tried not to think about the fact that he hadn't withdrawn his hand. *"O."*

He grinned. *"C."*

Carly snorted. "This isn't working."

"Poor loser."

"I'm not playing a game where every word is about sex."

"What are you talking about?" His phony innocence was too much.

"You know darn well what word you were aiming for."

"What's wrong with *cocoon?*"

She opened her mouth. Nothing came out.

However, a loud moan came from the room, and then two more.

Rick turned to peer into the room. "Shit, I didn't know Tony had so much stamina."

"Hey, don't look."

His jaw slackened. "Oh, my, God. What are they—?"

She twisted around. All she could see was a lump of sheets.

Rick chuckled. "Made you look."

She swung back around, more embarrassed than she'd care to admit. "That was so juvenile."

"Remember that time we spied on old man—what was his name? Clemmens? Clampett?"

She smiled at the memory. "Homer Clemson."

"We thought he was making moonshine in that shed in the woods. Turns out he had a stash of *Penthouse* and *Playboy* magazines."

"I never ran so fast in my entire life."

"He was mad enough to use that switch on us. His entire bald head was as red as a tomato."

"I didn't think he could even move that quickly."

"Yeah, especially not with that big belly of his." Rick shifted again, angling more toward her. "You know that really wasn't a switch, don't you?"

"What do you mean?"

"We were kids. So of course we assumed it was a switch. But it was a whip. One of those S and M devices."

"No way." She knew his wife, his kids. They all went to her father's church.

"Yep."

"How do you know?"

"I snuck back to the shed the next evening."

"And you didn't tell me?"

He ran the pad of his thumb across her wrist. "You wouldn't have had a clue what any of that stuff was. It took me a day or two to figure it all out."

"You went back more than once?"

He winced.

"What? Is it your eye?"

"My thumb."

She picked up his hand. It was so large compared to hers, and his fingers were so long and lean they prompted totally unacceptable thoughts. "It looks a little swollen," she said and let go.

"At least it isn't throbbing anymore. It's really okay. I just bumped it. How's the shiner coming?"

She peered closer. "Not too bad. But I doubt you'll escape the black-and-blue phase."

"This is definitely not how I planned to enjoy my vacation."

She sighed. "Yeah, I know what you mean."

"Hey." He nudged her with his elbow.

"What?"

"Being stuck out here doesn't have to be a total waste of time. We could make out."

"Right." Her pulse quickened, and she moved away before he could sense her excitement.

He used a knuckle to lift her chin. "How much trouble can we get into out here?"

"Just as much as we could in there."

"Ah, the adventurous type." He brushed her cheek with the back of his hand. "Your skin is so incredibly soft."

She moistened her suddenly parched lips. He shifted, and she moved over to accommodate him. It looked like an invitation she belatedly realized when he drew his legs up and stretched them out beside her.

"Rick, we can't both fit on this thing. We'll break it."

"No way. You're barely over a hundred pounds," he said, his face so close their breath mingled. He put his hand on her belly. "You're round and flat in all the right places."

She had every intention of swatting his hand away, but when he slowly moved his palm over her ribcage, she only sucked in a breath.

"We have only a few more days, Carly." He kissed the side of her neck, moved his hand dangerously close to her right breast. "Why are we wasting all this time?"

What was a moment of pleasure compared to peace of mind? "Because we're both too sensible to get ourselves—ooh."

He'd nipped her earlobe with his teeth again.

"Rick..."

He used the tip of his tongue to trace the shell of her ear. "On vacation, nothing counts," he whispered and moved his hand higher, just under her breast.

She knew she should object. Push his hand away. But she couldn't seem to deny herself the warmth spreading throughout her body, the dampness growing between her thighs.

"Kiss me, Carly." He brushed his lips over hers, slowly, teasingly.

She swallowed. *On vacation, nothing counts.* Hadn't she and Ginger arrived at the same conclusion? Sex here in the middle of the Caribbean was more like having a really awesome dream, like some wild fantasy that disappeared as soon as you hit home base. So what if it was Rick?

He slid his tongue along the seam of her lips, picked

up her limp hands and pulled them around his waist. She couldn't think anymore. All she could do was feel his warmth, the muscular ridges of his back. The sexy and desirable way he made her feel stole her breath.

Briefly, she let her eyes drift shut. "Someone might see us," she whispered against his mouth.

"Too dark," he murmured, sucking her lower lip between his teeth. He drew back and smiled. "Did you see the moon?"

She shook her head

"Look. Coming up over those palms toward the mountain."

She glanced over her shoulder to see the large golden orb. It seemed incredibly close. Almost as if she could reach out and touch it.

He took a nip of her chin. "Did I tell you full moons make me crazy?"

"What's your excuse the rest of the time?"

"I'm serious." He grabbed her arm and started nibbling it below her elbow, then worked his way up.

Carly giggled. "Stop."

He cupped a hand over her mouth and bit her on the neck when she struggled. "Go ahead. Scream."

She shoved his hand aside. "Don't tempt me." She glanced inside, fortunately saw nothing and quickly looked away.

"What's going on in there?"

"I don't know. Look for yourself."

"I'd rather do this." He kissed her again, his mouth hungrier this time, more demanding.

She couldn't breathe. Didn't care. She ran her palm

up his chest, over his hardened nipple, liking the feel of it against her palm.

He reached behind her, up under the shirt and she felt a tug on her bikini top, and then it was loose and sliding down her breasts, falling to her waist. When he drew back and slipped the shirt's top button out of the hole, she didn't stop him. He continued to unfasten the rest, and she just sat there, numb, excited, trying not to tremble.

When he was through, he pushed the front of the shirt aside and stared down at her bare breasts, his lips slightly parted, his nostrils flaring. He touched the tip of her nipple with his finger and then lightly drew circles around the hardening bud.

She shivered, and he looked up to meet her eyes.

A slow, sexy smile lifted his lips. "You're perfect," he whispered.

From the grassy area down below, a woman called out to her friend to meet her in the lobby bar. Afraid she could be seen, Carly pressed her chest against his. He groaned and drew her closer still, his restless hands roaming her back, delving beneath the elastic of her bikini bottoms.

"Someone will see—"

"No, they won't." Rick pressed a hot damp kiss on her neck. "We're too high up."

He drew back to stare at her breasts, flicking one nipple with the pad of his thumb. And then he lowered his head, and touched it with his tongue.

It was as if someone had shrink-wrapped her insides. She got all tight and hot and tingly. When he sucked her nipple into his mouth, she moaned softly, cupping the back of his head with her hands, encouraging him to use more pressure.

He obliged, and then took her hand and urged her to touch him through his swim trunks. He was hard and swollen, and after a few seconds she didn't hesitate to maneuver her hand under his elastic waistband until she could wrap her hand around him.

His silky hardness filled her palm, filled her with a fevered longing that erased all doubt. The tip was damp from an escaped bead of moisture and she used her forefinger to explore the smooth sleek skin.

Groaning, he worked his hand under the elastic leg of her bikini and found her wet heat. She jerked at the unfamiliar feel of his probing fingers and clenched her muscles. Slowly he slid his finger inside her. She clenched tighter. He raised his mouth from her breasts and captured her lips.

Light from inside the room flickered on, illuminating them. Reluctantly she broke the kiss. Growling his frustration, Rick reached around her and pulled the aloha shirt up over her shoulders, shielding her from view.

"Shitty timing," he said, shooting a glance over his shoulder. "But at least they're getting ready to leave."

"Do you think they saw us?"

"No way." He looked at her and smiled.

Helplessly, Carly stared back, still clutching his arms as if they were a life support. If this was a mistake, it was too late. She'd already gone over the edge. She needed him to pull her back.

The light went off, and Rick kissed her briefly and

then got up. "Okay, they're gone," he said, helping her to her feet.

She wrapped the shirt tightly around her, catching her bikini bra before it fell to the floor. He opened the sliding door and let her go in first. She remembered to grab the ice bucket.

Once they got inside and he turned on a lamp, she experienced a moment of awkwardness. She distracted herself by peering at his eye. It looked pretty good, considering. "Don't forget to put ice on that again."

Amusement danced in his face. "Not likely. I'll have you to remind me," he said and went to the dresser and pulled out the top drawer.

His trunks rode low on his slim hips, below his tan line, and she swallowed, remembering the long hard feel of him in her hand. He got something out of the drawer and then turned toward her. He held a foil packet.

She moistened her lips. Either she went for it or ran for cover. It was now or never.

On vacation, nothing counts.

She opened her shirt and shrugged out of it. Rick's appreciative gaze boosted her confidence, and she eagerly tossed the shirt aside. He dropped the foil packet on the bed and took her in his arms.

Still hard, he pressed his hips against her, slanting his mouth over hers, feverishly taking all she had to give. They were close enough to the bed that they sort of fell onto it, the process of getting there a blur. He needed little encouragement to get out of his trunks and then he hooked his fingers over her bikini bottoms and yanked them down.

He hesitated, taking a moment to simply stare at her, and miraculously she didn't feel the slightest embarrassed. She reached out and touched him, with only one finger, lightly on the silky tip, and he let out a low growl and pushed her backwards until she lay across the bed.

Greedily he suckled her breasts, ran his hands over her belly, down her thighs. She tried to reach for him again but he wouldn't let her. He just kept giving her pleasure, touching her in the most perfect way.

When he gently spread her thighs, her eagerness stunned her. Not a single qualm gave her pause. She closed her eyes and let his probing fingers ready her. She was so wet and slick she could have taken him without any trouble.

"Carly?"

Languidly she opened her eyes.

Rick smiled and brushed the hair off her damp cheeks. "Don't move a muscle."

Her heart thudded. "Where are you—"

He didn't have to answer. He'd already unwrapped the condom and, holding her breath, she watched him sheathe himself. He positioned himself between her thighs and then kissed her, before easing his thick hardness inside her. She clutched the sheets as he began to enter her, the feeling unfamiliar after so long but welcome. He whispered her name, and then plunged deep inside.

RICK SAT on the beach and watched the sun come up. Not a normal occurrence for him to be awake this early but since he'd barely slept three hours last night he figured what the hell. He only wished Carly was sitting beside him.

Last night had been incredible. Not just the sex, although the third time they'd made love had been an experience entirely off the map. But it was the connection he'd felt with her that had really blown him away. As if they'd been together a lifetime. As if they shared the same soul.

He checked his watch and realized he'd been sitting at the water's edge for over an hour. It had taken everything he had not to call her room and wake her. Hell, she'd only left him four hours ago but he already missed her. He got to his feet, and he kicked a shell toward the water lapping the sand.

"What are you doing here?"

He jerked around. "Me? What about you?"

Carly gave him a wry smile. She had on tiny white shorts, her legs already starting to turn golden. She looked so damn good he thought he'd burst. "I couldn't sleep."

"I know. I had the same problem." He reached for her hand and she went to him without hesitation. "Hungry?"

"What did you have in mind?" she asked, tilting her head back to look up at him, the suggestion in her eyes heating his blood.

"Looks like I created a monster." He kissed the tip of her nose, pulled her against him.

"Rick?"

He held his breath. God, he hoped he didn't hear regret in her voice. "Yeah?"

"After breakfast could we, um..." She shrugged,

smiled. "Ginger and Tony are going water-skiing this morning. It'd be a shame to waste our room."

He grinned. "Sweetheart, you just read my mind."

CARLY CURLED UP against his warm body and refused to open her eyes. It was morning. She could tell light was streaming into her room. But today was their last day and she didn't want it to end. The past two days with Rick had been more than she could have hoped for.

He moved, and immediately reached around to cup her bottom with his hands. "Hey," he said sleepily.

"Hey back." She loved the feel of her breasts pressed against his back and circled her arms around him to finger his nipples.

His low throaty chuckle vibrated right through her. "You haven't had enough, eh?"

"What?" she asked innocently, yet unable to keep from smiling.

"Ah, so that's the way it is." He rolled over onto his back and caught her wrist. "You wanna play coy."

She laughed. "I just wanna play."

His gaze lowered to her mouth and he pulled her on top of him. Surprised at how hard he'd already gotten, she moved her hips and smiled at the look of helplessness in his eyes.

"You asked for it," he whispered and cupped her nape.

"Yes, I did."

He kissed her, deeply, feverishly, and she kissed him back, hoping to chase the sudden and unexpected melancholy away. Tomorrow the fantasy ended.

GINGER SETTLED onto the barstool and sighed. "I can't believe we leave today."

"I can't believe we got kicked out of our room so early."

Carly asked the bartender for orange juice and three cherries, and then covered her mouth as she yawned widely.

"We didn't get kicked out. Noon is checkout time." Ginger licked the whipped cream off the strawberry daiquiri the bartender had automatically served her, and then grinned. "It's good for you to get out from under the covers. You need the sunshine."

"You should talk. Besides, we're sitting in a bar."

Ginger ignored Carly's dry observation and glanced over her shoulder. "Tony should have been here ten minutes ago. Have you seen Rick yet?"

Carly shook her head and then promptly picked up the orange juice the bartender set down. Her mouth was as dry as the Mojave Desert. How could this all be ending? She'd just had the most perfect three days of her entire life.

Ginger glanced at her watch. "I know they've checked out already. I saw Rick in the gift shop."

"When?"

"About a half hour ago."

Carly frowned. He'd said he would meet her down here. God, she hated the disappointment and apprehension twisting the insides of her stomach. Today was goodbye. She'd known it was coming. Had to come.

Ginger shot her a curious look. "What's going on with you two, anyway?"

"What do you mean?"

"You know, plans for you visiting him, or him visiting you."

Carly shook her head. "No plans. This was it. We had our fun."

"Right."

"Remember the ground rules?"

Ginger gave her an annoyingly smug smile. "You're full of it."

"I like you better when you're self-absorbed."

"Funny." Ginger twisted around. "Where the hell is he?"

She gave a casual shrug. "Maybe they've already headed for the airport."

Ginger's stricken face made Carly regret her words. "He wouldn't leave without saying goodbye—" Ginger bit her lower lip "—or asking for my phone number."

Alarm bells went off in Carly's head. She hoped she didn't sound or look like Ginger. Especially after all her posturing with Rick about this being a fling, and nothing more. Of course it was different with them....

She cringed. No, it wasn't. God, she would *not* go there. They'd had a vacation fling. End of story.

"Don't say it. I know." Ginger jabbed at the daiquiri with her straw, her face a mask of misery. "It's supposed to be a no-strings-attached one-week fling. But we really clicked, you know? We may have something." She paused and met Carly's eyes. "Don't look at me like that."

"Like what?" Heat crept into her face. She'd actually been thinking about Rick.

"You know like what. And don't even think about giving me a sermon because—" Ginger's attention was drawn to something behind Carly, and she slid off the stool. "There's Tony. Rick's with him," she said as she waved them over.

Carly took a deep breath. Her heart beat way too fast.

As soon as the two men got there, Ginger lifted her chin for Tony's kiss.

He hesitated, and then gave her a light peck. Hurt flickered in her eyes, but she pasted on a smile. "You guys wanna have a drink?" She turned to signal the bartender.

Tony gently took her by the arm. "We don't have time. We're going to the airport."

Carly's gaze flew to Rick. He'd come up alongside her and put a familiar hand on the small of her back. His eyes stayed trained on Tony.

"But your flight isn't for another three hours," Ginger said, her voice unnaturally high.

Tony pushed a hand through his hair. "Yeah, I know."

Ginger's panicked face was too painful to watch, and Carly looked away. No way would she come off looking pathetically wistful like that. By tomorrow she'd be back in Oroville. Back to reality. She'd probably never see Rick again. Or if she did, it would just be for a weekend....

No. No. No.

No weekends. No wishing.

"Are you two out of your room yet?" Rick asked. She nodded, glancing over at Ginger and Tony.

They were whispering to each other and not paying any attention to them. "Can you believe how fast this week went?" Carly said, trying to sound nonchalant.

"It sucks, doesn't it?"

"Yeah," she said. "But I'm looking forward to starting work."

"Not me. I'd stay another week if I could." He leaned in closer, his breath tickling her ear. "What do you say? Let's go see if they have another room for the week."

She laughed. He sounded serious. Of course he wasn't, and even if he was the idea was out of the question. "It was fun," she said breezily in an amazingly matter-of-fact tone. "But reality calls."

Unsmiling, he studied her for a long uncomfortable moment, and then he took his airline ticket out of the breast pocket of his green aloha shirt and reviewed the itinerary.

Even though he seemed at ease, she had the feeling he felt as awkward as she did. But for the life of her, she couldn't think of anything to say.

He put away the ticket and looked over at the other two. "Hey, Tony, we'd better get outside. Our cab's probably waiting."

Carly mentally winced. This was really goodbye.

"Yeah, okay." Tony gave Ginger a hug.

She said something to him, and when he didn't respond, she slipped a piece of paper into his shirt pocket.

Rick smiled at Carly as he adjusted his carry-on strap over his shoulder. "Carly, I—"

She put a finger to his lips to silence him. Ignoring

the queasy feeling in her stomach, she smiled back. "Take care, and travel safely."

"You, too." Hurt and indecision flickered in his eyes, and then he leaned over and kissed her cheek.

Rick turned away before he said something stupid, and walked alongside Tony to the circular drive to meet their cab. This was a shitty way to say goodbye. He'd almost given in and told her he wanted to call her if it was okay.

Until she'd cut him off. Dismissed him.

What was up with that?

He didn't need that kind of attitude. Hell, even after the last few days, nothing had changed. She didn't want anything from him. All she wanted was her nice safe little world in Oroville. That's why he wouldn't look back. No way he'd give her the satisfaction. Assuming she was even still there.

He probed the bruised spot under his eye. It was in a lot better shape than his ego.

9

CARLY HAD just put the box of oatmeal back into the cupboard when her father entered the kitchen. "Morning, Daddy. I didn't know you were still here."

He yawned and then gave her a weary smile. "I was up late writing my sermon for tomorrow."

She got out a mug and poured his coffee, adding a scant teaspoon of sugar and low-fat milk. At fifty he worried about adding pounds to his lean frame. Carly used to tease him about being vain. Wanting to stay fit and be healthy was not the same as vanity, he'd informed her.

"What's it going to be about?" she asked, reclaiming the seat at the table she'd just left. She still had fifteen minutes before she had to leave for town.

"Chastity."

"Oh, yes, good topic." She swallowed around the lump of guilt in her throat as she set the mug in front of him. Far worse than the guilt were thoughts of Rick. No matter how hard she tried not to think about him, he popped into her thoughts at the oddest times.

"Thank you, honey," her father said, picking up his coffee and taking a sip. "I know everyone has heard numerous sermons on chastity before, but I'm going to expand the subject. Discuss the difference between being physically and mentally chaste.''

He paused, and Carly felt as if she were twelve again, when it seemed he knew her every misdeed just by looking at her. She'd never been able to lie to him, no matter how small the fib.

Then he smiled and reached across the table to cover her hand with his. ''Have I told you how nice it is to have you home again?''

She nodded, the guilt giving way to a warm contentment. ''I think you may have mentioned it a few times.''

He laughed. ''Yes, I suppose I have. Your mother was especially lonely those six years you were away.''

''It wasn't as if I didn't come home often.''

''Not the same, honey.''

The phone rang and he frowned at the digital microwave clock.

''I'll get it.'' Carly jumped up even though she knew it was probably for him. She had to have been the only teenager for a hundred miles whose father had gotten more phone calls than she. Pastor Ray was always available for his congregation, and sometimes the calls just didn't stop.

''Pastor Ray's residence.''

''Carly?''

''Ginger?''

''Yeah. I hope I'm not interrupting anything.''

Carly made a motion to her father that it was for her, and watched thankfully as he got up and took his coffee out onto the back porch to watch the magpies raid the birdfeeder. This was the second phone call from Ginger in the week since they'd been back, and judging from her morose tone, the topic would be the same.

"I have ten minutes before I have to leave. What's up?"

"He still hasn't called."

Carly leaned a hip against the counter and kept an eye on her father through the window. "We already talked about this."

"I know, but you don't understand. It wasn't just about sex. It was supposed to be, but it wasn't."

Carly struggled for a moment, considering the wisdom of total honesty. "I don't want to upset you, but maybe for Tony that's all it was."

Silence.

"Ginger? I'm sorry. I had to say it."

"I know." Her voice was small, and Carly thought she heard a sniffle. "You're probably right."

"But then again, he still may call. Getting back from vacation can be hectic."

"That's true." Ginger's voice lightened. "He'd mentioned that he almost had to cancel his vacation because of his workload."

Carly wanted to kick herself for offering false hope. Why couldn't she have let well enough alone? Why did she have this compulsion to smooth things over, make things right for everyone? She'd known that last day at the lobby bar that Tony had no intention of calling Ginger. For him, the fun and games were over. Ginger would have seen it, too, if she hadn't been so starry-eyed.

"That said," Carly added, "there's also a good

chance he won't call. Who knows? He could even have a girlfriend.''

"Tony isn't like that."

Carly decided not to point out that Ginger really didn't know him. "I'm just saying that you shouldn't wait around for his call. It might not happen."

Ginger sighed. "You could call Rick and find out about Tony for me."

Carly nearly dropped the phone. "Are you crazy?"

"Why not? I bet you guys have talked a dozen times already."

"Guess again."

"Really?"

"Really."

"Have you talked to him at all?"

"Nope. That wasn't part of the deal." Carly hated these calls from Ginger. Most of the time she could distract herself from replaying those last days with Rick. Darn, it wasn't supposed to smart like this. "I don't even know his number."

"You know what city he lives in. He's probably listed. Use me as an excuse to call."

"No, Ginger, absolutely not."

"I'd do it for you, Carly. You know I would. In a heartbeat."

The back door opened, and her father came in and headed for the coffeepot.

"Look, I have an appointment in town. I really have to go."

"Think about it, okay? And call me later." Ginger's desperation came through loud and clear.

"I will. Later this evening."

"Thanks, Carly, you're the best." She hung up and Carly did, too, but with the sinking feeling that Ginger had misunderstood.

"Problem?" Her dad peered at her over the rim of his mug.

"Not really." She shrugged. "A girlfriend is having man trouble."

He broke out in a smile. "Part of growing up, my dear. In three months she won't remember his name."

Carly forced a smile and nodded. Pastor Ray was right about most things, but he'd missed something here. She and Ginger were already grown up, and it would be a very long time before either of them forgot their Caribbean vacation. Or the men they'd met there.

Carly, who prided herself on never swearing, cursed under her breath. Because damn if she wasn't thinking about calling Rick.

"DON'T YOU look pretty today?" Nate Brown, the only druggist who'd worked at Dagwoods Drugs and Sundry since Carly could remember, greeted her the same way he had for the past twenty-something years.

"Thank you, Mr. Brown." She smiled as she placed a bottle of aspirin in her basket, even though she knew exactly what she looked like, and 'pretty' definitely wasn't it. She'd barely slept four hours in each of the past three nights. Ever since Ginger had asked her to call Rick.

The idea was absurd, Carly had concluded, and she definitely would do no such thing, but Ginger had been desperate and relentless. And Carly felt awful for her.

"I heard you went on one of those Caribbean vacations a couple of weeks ago,'' Mr. Brown said, peering at her over the same wire spectacles he'd worn for twenty years.

"Yes, I had a wonderful time.'' Of course, everyone knew she'd been away at college, probably even knew about the stomach virus she had for two weeks during junior year. Little escaped these people. Especially when it came to Pastor Ray's only daughter.

"Glad to see you didn't get too much sun. Not good for your skin, you know,'' he said, peering over his glasses at her. "Where exactly did you go? My sister-in-law Martha visited St. Thomas three years ago. All she talked about was the shopping.''

Carly mentally shuddered. She hated to lie, but no way would she tell anyone where she really went, even though she doubted anyone in Oroville had ever heard of Club Nirvana.

"It wasn't a well known island. I doubt you've heard of it.'' She picked up a tube of cream that claimed to be a miracle for dry skin. "Do you know anyone who's tried this?''

He chuckled. "Young thing like you doesn't need that.''

"I don't know about that. I'm getting up there.''

He snorted. "Why I remember when you were in diapers. You hated the things and always tried to pull them off.'' He cupped a hand to the side of his mouth. "Some folks around here were afraid you'd end up like one of them nudists.''

She laughed. That one she hadn't heard before.

Behind her, deep rumbling laughter sent a shiver down her spine. The sound reminded her of Rick. But it couldn't be. Her mind was obviously playing tricks on her.

Mr. Brown smiled at whoever was behind her. "Carly, I have a surprise for you. You have an old friend visiting town. Remember Agatha Weaver's grandson?"

Carly held her breath and slowly turned around.

"You do remember Rick, don't you?" Mr. Brown asked.

A slow taunting smile lifted Rick's lips. "Hello, Carly."

She couldn't speak. Couldn't move.

He took a step toward her, and she quickly put out her hand. He took it and pulled her close. Before she could react, he lightly kissed her cheek and then stepped back.

"Long time no see," he said, his gaze fixed on hers. "You're looking good."

"Thank you." Heat stung her cheeks. "You, too."

"If I hadn't told you who he was, would you have recognized him?" Mr. Brown stepped down from behind the pharmacy counter and came to stand by the register. "He sure has changed, hasn't he?"

"Yup," Carly agreed. "He's much taller."

Mr. Brown chuckled. "Well, son, are you ready for me to ring up your merchandise?"

"I think so."

Carly looked at his empty hands.

"If I forgot anything, I'll go next door and borrow it from Carly." He grinned as he walked up beside her, picked up a pack of breath mints from a display and tossed it on the counter next to a package of razor blades and toothpaste.

Her chest tightened. "Next door?"

"My grandmother's house."

"But it's been closed up."

He pulled a wallet out of his back pocket and grinned. "Not anymore."

"But—" She glanced at Mr. Brown. He was busy using his magnifying glass to read the sticker prices. Her insides were jumping around like firecrackers. She willed a calmness she was far from feeling. "Are you getting it ready to be sold?"

A spark of devilment in his eye made her sorry she'd even shown the interest. "Why? You interested in buying?"

She shrugged. "Maybe."

"Ah, that would be nice. Right next door to Mommy and Daddy."

She glared at him, tempted to tell him to screw off. Mindful of Mr. Brown's presence, she calmed down and smiled. "Well, it was nice seeing you, but I do have to run." She glanced at Mr. Brown. "I'll have Minnie ring my things up at the front register."

"Okey-dokey."

"See you around, Carly," Rick called after her.

Not if she could help it.

RICK WATCHED her leave. She wasn't happy about seeing him. Not that he'd expected her to be. God forbid he should mess up her safe little world.

"Nice girl that Carly Saunders. Glad she came back

to Oroville. Most young people don't these days. They all take off for the big cities.''

''That's where all the jobs are,'' Rick said absently, his mind on Carly. She looked different. Maybe it was the long baggy shorts and shapeless plaid shirt that made her look—not frumpy exactly, but—hell, she looked frumpy. Nothing like the woman he'd spent time with in the Caribbean.

Mr. Brown snorted as he started to ring up Rick's purchases. ''Yup, that's what they say. Going to look for jobs that pay real money.''

It took Rick a second to recall their conversation. ''Can't blame them for wanting to get ahead.''

''Nope, but they don't think it through. Like how much those city houses and everything else cost. Before you know it, they're calling home for money.'' His white brows drew together as he studied the register. ''Your total is three-eighty. Tell me you can beat that price in…where is it you say you're from?''

''Los Angeles.''

''Holy smoke, I heard a lot about prices out there.''

''Yeah.'' Rick dug into his pocket. ''No joke.''

''So how long are you planning on staying in Oroville?''

''I'm not sure.'' Rick handed him a bill. ''Maybe a week or two.''

''You'll be selling your grandma's house, I suspect.''

Obviously the older man hadn't been listening to him and Carly. Just as well. ''I don't know.''

He had no idea why he'd said that. Of course he'd sell. Assuming anyone wanted to buy it. Brown was right. People weren't exactly lining up to move to Oroville.

Mr. Brown packaged Rick's stuff and then handed him his change. "We all sure miss Agatha. Even as ornery as she'd gotten in her golden years." He smiled. "No matter what, she never talked bad about anybody."

"I miss her, too." A wave of melancholy swept him. Her letters had never stopped, even when he'd been too self-absorbed to reply.

To her, he hadn't been an inconvenience or merely a social responsibility, as he had been to his parents. She'd truly loved him, and had been interested in his life. It had been a surprise at first when she'd left him the house. But on reflection, he understood the affection she felt for him. He only wished he'd realized sooner. Before she'd passed away. Before he'd wasted so much time trying to please his parents.

Rick pocketed the change and dug out his car keys. "Thanks, Mr. Brown. For everything."

CARLY FOUND a spot close to the side door of Milton's Market and parked her Honda Civic. She glanced around before getting out. Only two other cars were in the lot, and she recognized both of them.

If she'd had her way, she wouldn't have come to town at all. But her mother had asked her to pick up some fresh produce and she could have hardly refused just because she didn't want to run into Rick.

Actually, she didn't know why she was worried. He'd probably gotten bored to death and already left town…although she had noticed a light on in the Weaver house last night and again early this morning. Not that she'd made a point of looking.

But it wasn't as if she could ignore that he was in town either. It had taken her the rest of the afternoon to get her breathing regulated after seeing him in the drugstore yesterday. The mere thought started her pulse racing again, and she took several deep breaths before glancing in the rearview mirror and then getting out of the car.

As soon as she entered the small market, she smelled the aroma of fresh-baked bread. Limited baking and cooking was still done in the back of the store and if you came in at the right day and time, you could get a whiff of Mrs. Fisher's buttery fried chicken.

Milton Fisher had opened his store over thirty years ago and, although a lot of Oroville's residents went to the Wal-Mart and Albertson's in Cedar City to do their major shopping these days, enough of them still patronized Milton's to keep the store in business.

Thank goodness, Carly thought as she grabbed a hand basket and started down the cereal and coffee aisle. While away at college, she'd sometimes dreamed about Mrs. Fisher's incredible cinnamon sticky buns.

She picked up some sugar and chamomile tea and then headed for the produce section. The bins looked as if they'd been recently stocked, brimming with bright shiny red apples and the latest summer melons.

"Everything looks delicious, Mr. Fisher," she called out as he appeared out of the stockroom, moping his balding head.

"Sure does."

At the sound of Rick's voice, she spun around.

He gazed at her as though he wanted to eat her up, and a slow smile curved his mouth.

"What are you doing here?" she muttered, angry with her traitorous body. One little look, one little smile and the tingling sensation had started in her belly and spread down between her thighs.

Mr. Fisher walked up in time to hear and gave her an odd look.

"Same as you. Admiring the produce." He smiled at Mr. Fisher. "I'll take a couple of tomatoes. Do we help ourselves?"

"Oh, sure." Mr. Fisher's rotund body hid the roll of plastic bags. He turned around and tore one off for Rick. "Would you like one?" Mr. Fisher asked Carly.

"Thank you." She took it, ignoring the curiosity in the older man's eyes, and gave her back to Rick as she made her selection.

Thank heavens it was Mr. Fisher out here and not Mrs. Fisher. He might be curious, but he wouldn't ask any questions. Mrs. Fisher would be giving her the third degree by now. Heck, if they had any questions about Rick, let them ask him themselves.

"The cantaloupes look pretty good, too." He was still behind her. How could he see the cantaloupes? "In fact, they look damn good."

She furtively glanced in his direction. He was staring at her butt. Her gaze immediately went to Mr. Fisher, who seemed to be hiding a smile as he ambled back toward the stockroom.

"I don't believe you." She wanted to tell him off, but held her tongue.

"What?"

Not trusting herself to speak, she threw the tomatoes into the basket with too much force.

"You're overreacting," he whispered.

"So it's my fault Mr. Fisher is probably asking his wife this very minute who you are and why I'm so mad I could smack you?"

"Exactly."

Carly hesitated, at a loss for words, and then she said, "Go to hell," for the first time in her life.

"DID YOU KNOW that Agatha's grandson is back in town?" Eileen Saunders peered out the kitchen window toward the house, where Rick was probably sitting right now, thinking up ways to make Carly's life miserable. "I meant to ask you yesterday morning when I saw a light on if you knew who was there."

Carly sighed. If only her mother had mentioned it sooner... And then what? Would Carly have stayed away from town? Hidden in her room until she thought he'd left?

"I ran into Mabel Crabtree at the butcher this afternoon and she told me it was Rick. I know you remember him." Her mother turned away from the window to look at Carly with a gentle smile. "You two were nearly inseparable the first summer he spent here."

"Inseparable?"

Her mother's eyes crinkled at the corners. They were the most stunning blue and Carly had wished since her childhood that she'd been blessed with such a unique color. "Yes, inseparable. You ate lunch together every day out in the woods and went swimming in the lake twice a day and—"

"Yeah, I remember." Carly missed the carrot she was peeling and caught the tip of her finger. "Damn it!"

"Carly Ann! What's the matter with you?"

"Sorry, Mom."

"I believe that's the first time I've heard you swear."

"It's not *that* bad a word." Carly's mood plummeted impossibly further. She never swore. That was one of the things Rick mentioned that he liked about her. What the heck did she care? Why was she even thinking about him?

"No, it's not," her mom agreed, much to Carly's surprise. "But it startled me. Is something wrong?"

"I guess being back is a little more of an adjustment than I anticipated."

"Are you sorry?"

Concerned she'd hurt her mother's feelings, Carly turned to her. "About coming back?"

Her mother nodded and took the carrot and peeler out of her hands and put them aside.

"Of course not."

"Come, let's sit down." She washed and dried her hands. "Dinner can wait."

Carly reluctantly followed her to the kitchen table. She hoped this wasn't going to be one of those heart-to-heart mother-and-daughter talks. Not that they had many. But right now wasn't the time. Carly's nerves were frayed at best.

They sat across from each other and Carly gazed at

her mother, marveling as she always did at how well her mother had aged. Of course she was only forty-seven, but still, with her shiny brown hair and smooth complexion, she looked more like forty. Carly hoped she aged that well.

"We never really talked about you coming back to Oroville, did we?"

The question took Carly by surprise. "I didn't see that there was anything to discuss."

Her mother smiled gently. "I only meant that your father and I are aware there were other options. Of course we love having you here with us, but we hoped you didn't feel obligated."

Carly gave her head an emphatic shake. "Not in the least. This is my home. I love Oroville. I'm excited about my teaching job, which, by the way, starts in two weeks. I've already completed the first semester's curriculum, handed it in and had it approved."

"Was there any doubt?" Pride shone in her mother's eyes. "That school is lucky to have you, and they know it."

"Not that you're biased or anything."

"Of course I am, but that's beside the point."

Carly laughed. "It is good to be home. Want some coffee?"

"Only if it's decaf. It's getting late."

She got up and checked the potatoes she'd put on to boil and then measured the coffee. "What time is Dad getting home?"

"Probably in an hour."

"I'll start frying the chicken in twenty minutes."

"Why don't you let me help?"

"Sit." She gave her mom a stern look. "I told you my work is all caught up and I'm making dinner. If I'm going to live here we're going to have to share the chores."

"All you need to do is keep up your room."

"Mom, I'm a grown woman."

"You're right."

A brief silence lapsed.

"You know to use a mixture of flour and cornstarch for the batter, don't you?"

Carly sighed. "Yes, Mother, I do."

"Well, okay…"

"Look, if you don't trust me—"

"Of course I do."

Smiling to herself, Carly turned back to the coffee. "Then just sit there and look pretty and we'll have a nice chat while I cook."

"Don't forget the corn. Your father loves corn on the cob with chicken and mashed potatoes. Oh, and the gravy." She stood. "I could make that."

"Mom."

She sat again. "I'll just sit here and look pretty."

"Good." Carly poured in the water and flipped on the coffeemaker. She got down two mugs and placed them on the counter just as she heard a knock at the back door.

She cocked her head to see who it was.

Rick.

He stood on the other side of the screen door. He'd changed into khaki cargo shorts and a worn powder-blue T-shirt that clung to his broad chest like a second skin and accentuated his golden-bronze tan.

Smiling, he held up a measuring cup. "May I borrow some sugar?" he said through the screen.

"No," she said, and slammed the wooden door shut.

10

"CARLY ANN Saunders!"

Carly cringed. How could she have forgotten her mother sitting right there behind her? That was the trouble with Rick. He made her crazy. Reason evaporated. Common sense melted away like spring snow.

Reluctantly she opened the door. The amusement on his face was almost more than she could take.

"Why do you need sugar?" she demanded. "I know you aren't baking."

"For my coffee."

"For goodness sake, Carly, that's Rick. Invite him in."

"He's in a hurry." Carly gave him a meaningful look that he blithely ignored.

"Thank you, Mrs. Saunders," he said, winking at Carly as he stepped past her.

"My, you've grown into a fine-looking young man. Hasn't he Carly?"

She wouldn't even look at him. His closeness alone had caused her tummy to flutter. "He still looks like the same old ugly toad to me."

Rick laughed and touched her chin before she could jerk away. "That's my girl."

Her mother shook her head, an inquisitive gleam in

her eye. "Not much has changed, I see. Come sit and have a cup of coffee with us. Carly just made some."

"Thanks, I'd like that."

Carly debated making an excuse to go upstairs. But that would leave Rick alone with her mom. No way.

"In fact, Carly's fixing dinner tonight. You'll have to stay and eat with us."

She gave him a warning look. If he said yes, he was toast....

"Thanks, I'd love to." He smiled at both women and took a chair across the table from Carly's mother, the seat right next to Carly's. "It's been a while since I've had a home-cooked meal." And then to Carly, he added, "You sure you know how to cook?"

Her mother laughed. "You two seem to have taken up right where you left off. What's it been, eleven, twelve years since you've seen each other?"

Rick glanced at Carly. "I guess Carly didn't tell you."

Her mother frowned. "What?"

Carly held her breath. She should have mentioned that she'd run into Rick on vacation. It wouldn't have been a big deal. Big coincidence maybe, but no big deal. Now it would be. Her stomach turned.

He held Carly's gaze for a moment. "Yesterday at Dagwoods and this afternoon at the market. I ran into her when I was picking up some groceries."

Her mother's brows went up. "Why didn't you tell me?"

Carly shrugged. "I just didn't think of it."

Eileen Saunders's brows came down, her expression speculative as she glanced from Rick to Carly.

"I figured Mr. Brown had already told you. He's the one who pointed Rick out to me. Guess he's slipping in the grapevine department."

"Now, now." Her mom tried unsuccessfully to hide a smile. "I'll get the coffee."

"No, I'm already up." Carly quickly started getting out mugs and spoons before her mother could argue. She kept an ear on the conversation while she poured the coffee and set out cream and sugar, her heart rate still not completely back to normal.

She owed Rick for keeping his mouth shut. He could have really made her squirm, but he hadn't. Still, he wasn't innocent. He had to know what his suddenly showing up would do to her.

"Carly, are you listening?"

"I'm sorry." She snapped out of her musings. "What did you say, Mom?"

"We were just talking about the new ski resort they're building outside of town. I told Rick you're pretty caught up for school and that you'd probably be able to take him up there for a tour."

Carly brought the coffee to the table. "I'd really love to, but you know how I hate high altitudes."

Her mother gave her a curious look before stirring cream into her coffee.

Okay, so it was a lame excuse.

Rick snorted. "How high is this place?"

"Nineteen miles up the mountain. Over nine thousand feet elevation." Carly passed him the cream and sugar.

"No, thanks, I drink it black."

Carly stared at him, waiting for what he'd just admitted to register. She had to press her lips together when the sheepish look finally crossed his face. She made a point of glancing over at the empty measuring cup he'd brought, but kept her mouth closed. She owed him at least that much.

Her mother seemed inordinately interested, glancing back and forth between Carly and Rick. "So, Rick, since Carly has elected to keep me in the dark about you, tell me about your plans for your grandmother's house."

He shrugged. "I haven't really decided yet."

"You mean you might stay?"

He gave a startled jerk. "No. Or, I mean, I doubt it."

Carly stared at him. He doubted it? Surely, he had no plans to stay in Oroville. Why didn't he just admit it?

"Of course I thought about selling it," he said, "but I figured the market is pretty soft around here."

"True, but if the ski resort takes off, no telling how it'll affect the market around here. Seth Parker, you probably don't remember him, but he owns the only real estate office this side of Cedar City. He's been buying up land close to town where it's commercially zoned. Probably speculating on what an influx of winter tourists will require. I've been thinking about that some myself. It sure would be a good time to start a small business."

Carly stared in awe at her mother. She was a bright, educated woman, but all she'd ever been was the pastor's wife. That was all she'd ever wanted to be.

Eileen smiled. "Why are you looking at me like that?"

Carly blinked and then picked up her mug and sipped, nearly burning her mouth. She set down the coffee. "Nothing. I, uh—nothing really."

"You probably think your old mother isn't cut out to start a business."

"No, of course not," Carly protested immediately. "I think you can do anything you want to do. I just didn't think you wanted to do anything different." She glanced at Rick, really wishing he wasn't here for this conversation. "I mean, you always seem busy doing things at the church and all."

"True, but now that I don't have you to look after, I have more time." She lifted one slim shoulder. "Frankly, I got a little bored after you left for college."

"But I'm back." Carly instantly regretted the childish response.

Her mother grinned. "And, fortunately, you now wash your own clothes."

"What kind of business did you have in mind?" Rick asked, diverting the conversation.

"Oh, I don't know, maybe something in the line of food. Homemade soups and desserts that could be packed. Or even a gift shop where they could pick up souvenirs. A lot of the women in town are very good at crafts."

Rick nodded. "A consignment shop could work. That way there's no up-front capital. Everyone gets paid once their products sell."

Carly's mind went into overdrive. First, the thought

of her mother as this sudden entrepreneur, and then Rick giving her business advice. What did archeologists know about business?

Her mother leaned forward with interest. "Excellent idea. I can't wait to bring it up at the garden club meeting."

Carly silently sipped her coffee, wondering if she'd somehow been transported to a parallel universe. The house looked the same, so did the people, but everyone had short-circuited.

She set down her empty mug. "While you two talk I'll start dinner."

"Let me know if you need help." Her mother turned back to Rick. "The accounting sounds simple enough."

"Absolutely. You could do it yourself. Maybe hire an accountant to file the quarterly taxes."

"What are you doing now, Rick? I thought you were going to study archeology like your folks?"

Carly had stood, but she hesitated, interested in his answer. She knew he hated talking about his job. Would he evade her mother as he had her?

"Yeah, I studied archeology," he said slowly, his tone reluctant, his gaze staying clear of Carly's.

Her mother leisurely sipped her coffee, waiting patiently for him to continue.

"Mind if I get a refill?" He started to get up.

"I'll get it." Carly grabbed the carafe off the counter and topped off his mug.

He didn't look pleased.

"So what exactly are you doing now, Rick?" she asked, and sat down again.

"Research mostly." Unsmiling, he met her gaze, in his eyes a silent warning to back off.

"What kind?" Carly felt something under the table, and she shifted her legs to the side.

Molly, the stray gray tabby they'd adopted during Carly's junior year in high school, was outside. Besides, she was the noisiest cat west of the Mississippi. If she was under the table, everyone would know it.

"I mean, is it archeological research? Is it for your parents? Or just—" She jerked when she felt it again. Something stroked up her leg. Warm skin. Soft, coarse hair.

"I'm sorry, but would you two excuse me?" Her mother rose from the table. "I hear your dad's phone in his study. I was hoping they'd let the answering machine pick it up, but whoever it is seems persistent."

Sighing, Carly got up, too. She knew she would get no more information out of him without her mother present. "I hope you like southern-fried chicken because that's the way I make it."

"Sounds great." He pushed back from the table. "Want some help?"

"No, thanks." She reached on tiptoes for a bowl on the top shelf of the cabinet.

He came up behind her and reached over her head, lingering before he grabbed the bowl. "You smell good," he whispered.

"Stop it." She backed up…right into him.

"You feel good, too," he said, his voice lowering.

"Rick…"

"Your mom's in the other room. I can hear her on the phone."

She took the bowl from him. "Either sit down or I'll put you to work." Her heart was pounding so hard she didn't know how she managed to get the words out coherently.

"Good. I want to help."

"May I please have some room?" She made the mistake of turning around.

He lifted her chin so that their mouths were inches apart. "I've thought a lot about you these past two weeks."

"No."

His mouth lifted in a slow smile. "No?"

"You can't think about me."

"Ah, I see." His thumb brushed the corner of her mouth. "Okay, I'll try not to."

She should pull away, but the longing in his eyes held her captive, made her remember their last night on the island. He'd rented a boat and they'd made love in the moonlight.

"What are you doing after dinner?" He ran the pad of his thumb across her lower lip.

Her tongue darted out to moisten it and made brief contact with his thumb. He tensed, moved closer until his heat touched her and spread like wildfire. Placing one hand on the counter, he leaned in closer until her breasts grazed his chest.

Vaguely she heard the grandfather clock in the living room chime, the front door open and close, the magpies outside squawking for—

The front door…

It had to be her father.

Carly jumped, banging her hip hard on the counter. "It's my dad. He's home."

Rick seemed unfazed and in no hurry to move. She gave him a helpful shove. He stumbled backwards, laughing. "Guess what? I bet they know you kiss boys now."

"Shut up." She patted her hair and straightened her blouse.

"Carly?" Her father's voice preceded his appearance by a second. He came into the kitchen with a frown. "I thought that was your voice." Noticing Rick, he smiled. "Hello."

The couple of times she'd used "shut up" as a child had earned her entire afternoons in her room. "Hi, Dad, you remember Rick, don't you?"

She couldn't have sounded guiltier if she tried. She forced a smile, waiting for her dad to respond.

"I'm sorry," he said, setting his briefcase on the floor and then extending his hand to Rick. "You look familiar but I can't quite place you."

"Rick Baxter, sir. Agatha Weaver's grandson."

Recognition lit his eyes. "Of course. It's been a long time. Good to see you." They shook hands and then Carly's father said, "I assume you're staying next door."

Rick nodded and they made small talk for a few minutes while Carly started dinner preparations. Absurdly, her hands shook as she poured flour from the sunflower-patterned ceramic canister and measured out some salt and pepper. When she had trouble opening a jar of olives for the salad, Rick took it from her and unscrewed the cap without missing a word of conversation.

"Carly," her dad said in a quiet voice, while glancing over his shoulder toward the hall, "I hear your mom on the phone. Before she comes out here I wanted to tell you we wouldn't be home for dinner. I hope that isn't a problem."

"But—" she looked over at Rick "—she knew I was frying chicken. She even invited Rick to stay."

Ray gave her an apologetic smile. "It's a surprise. She doesn't know I'm taking her out to that place she likes in Cedar City."

"Oh."

"Honey, any other time I'd cancel," he said, glancing ruefully at the food she'd set out on the counter. "But it's our anniversary."

"Uh, Dad, I hate to tell you, but your anniversary isn't until October."

He laughed, his brown eyes sparkling, and somehow looking younger than he had just this morning. "Not that one. Today is the anniversary of when we first met thirty years ago. I bet she thinks I forgot."

Carly chuckled. That cinched it. This had to be a parallel universe. "The anniversary of when you met?"

"That's terrific." Rick grinned. "She'll be bowled over."

"I hope so." He put a finger to his lips when the silence down the hall suggested Eileen had gotten off the phone. "I'm sure Rick will help you eat that chicken."

Before Carly could inform them both that everything could wait for tomorrow, her mom appeared.

"Hi, honey, I didn't know you were home." She gave her husband a kiss on the cheek. "Carly has a surprise for you. She's making dinner."

"And I have a surprise for you," he said, sliding an arm around her waist and turning her back around toward the hall.

"But..." Her bewildered gaze went to Carly before he steered her toward their bedroom. "What are you...?"

Her voice faded into a delighted giggle right before they heard the bedroom door close.

Carly stared after them, shaking her head.

"That's really great."

She turned to Rick. "What's great?"

"That they still act that way."

"Like children?"

He made a face. "No, like two adults who are still in love with each other after thirty years."

She sighed, and looked toward the hall again. "It's not their usual behavior."

"Don't forget that you were away for a few years. They had time and space to rekindle the old romance."

"That's ridiculous."

"Oh, excuse me. I forgot." He picked out a cherry tomato she'd put in a bowl. "Parents don't have sex."

"Mine sure don't," she said, but couldn't get it out without laughing. "Okay, let's drop the subject. Some things children, even adult children, should never have to think about."

"Yeah, I know." He looked thoughtfully out the window. "I wish my parents acted like that. I think the last time my mother had an orgasm was when she discovered an Egyptian urn dating back to King Tut's era."

Carly snorted. "Now look who's being naive."

"Nope. That's the sad and unvarnished truth. You know, I think archeology is the only thing they have in common."

"And you."

"Yeah."

She didn't like his derisive tone. "Sounds as if you're on the outs with them."

"Wrong. They'd have to give a shit about me first."

She stared at him. He looked serious. "For goodness sake, Rick, of course they care about you."

"They should never have been parents." He shrugged. "I finally accepted that, and I don't hold it against them. They kept me well clothed and fed, and I had the best education my feeble brain allowed."

She didn't know quite what to say. He looked so at peace, not just resigned, but totally accepting. She turned off the potatoes and got out the foil. "When did you come to this conclusion?"

"You know how I used to get pissed off about being ditched for the summer? I'd try to make them feel guilty so they'd take me along to the next dig. They'd give in and take me for a token two weeks and then the whole dance would start again." He snatched the canister of flour out of her reach. "Why are you putting everything away?"

"You heard my dad. They're going out to dinner."

"What about us?"

"Mom invited you. I didn't."

"Come on, Carly. I've been so well-behaved." He got in her face and gave her big cow eyes. "And it would be my first home-cooked meal in I don't know how long."

She laughed. "Save the guilt trips for your parents."

Holding her gaze, he solemnly shook his head. "I don't waste my time that way anymore. Either someone wants to be with me or they don't."

Touched by his honesty Carly stared back for a long thoughtful moment, and then she silently drained the potatoes and started to mash them.

11

RICK PUT AWAY the last dish and hung the towel up to dry. Too late he realized he really shouldn't have eaten that last piece of chicken—his fourth piece, along with mashed potatoes, a gallon of country gravy, two cobs of buttered corn and a couple of the biscuits Carly had made at the last minute. He'd finally put the brakes on when she'd offered the apple pie, but the night was still young.

He watched her rearrange the refrigerator to accommodate the leftovers, admiring the way her bottom filled out the ugly baggy shorts when she bent over.

"I think that'll do it." She stuffed in the container of gravy and then straightened. "I left the whipped cream up front in case you change your mind about the pie."

Groaning, he flattened a hand against his belly. "I can barely move as it is."

Her lips lifted in a mysterious smile.

"However, I could be easily motivated." Guessing at her thoughts, he waggled his brows up and down.

She shook her head and tried to suppress a smile. "Incorrigible."

"And that's one of my better qualities."

Her expression sobered. "Stop that."

"What?"

"Making disparaging remarks about yourself."

"It was a joke."

She didn't say anything, but the disbelief in her eyes as she turned away to wipe off the counter spoke volumes.

"Christ, Carly, don't make anything out of what I told you about my relationship with my parents." They'd had a nice talk over dinner. He'd been relieved she hadn't pried, just listened. Not that he'd talked all that much about himself, but more than he did with most people.

"I'm not. I just—I don't know." She pushed the coffeemaker back against the wall.

He wasn't going to take the bait. She probably expected him to press her for an explanation. No way. He was done talking.

She dried her hands and then reached behind to untie her apron. Her breasts jutted out, round and perfectly sized, the nipples hard enough to show through the fabric, and he had an instant reaction.

Quickly he turned away and pretended interest in something outside the window. The Saunders had a great backyard. An elm shaded a redwood picnic table and benches, and at least a half dozen pines hosted handmade birdfeeders.

Near the vegetable garden was a white stone birdbath, empty now in the setting sun, but earlier it had been crowded with robins, doves and blue jays. It was still warm though, a perfect summer evening. It was a shame they hadn't thought to eat outside....

"I've got an idea."

Carly picked up her iced tea. "What?"

"Let's go for a swim."

"Now?"

"Yeah."

She looked at him as if he'd gone mad. "It'll be dark soon."

"So?"

"Some other time."

"Come on. We used to go at dusk all the time. What happened to your sense of adventure?"

She narrowed her gaze. "You're the one who didn't like swimming in the dark. You were convinced some kind of monster lived in the lake."

"I was only messing with you," he lied. Those slimy weeds on the bottom that crawled around his legs had felt like tentacles to him.

She grinned. "One time you thought a snake had bitten you, remember? Turns out it was a gnarled branch."

"Yeah, yeah. Go get your swimsuit."

Her smile faded. "I don't think so."

"Okay, skip the swimsuit. Skinny-dipping sounds better, anyway."

She rolled her gaze toward the ceiling.

"Come on, Carly." He grabbed her hand and tugged her close. "No one has to know we went swimming together."

"I don't care if—"

"Liar."

She glared at him, her cute little chin lifting in indignation. "Contrary to your unfounded opinion, I do not worry about what people think."

He shouldn't press. It would be a shame to let the evening end on a sour note. Besides, she'd back away from him and he liked having her this close, the subtle scent of her vanilla shampoo filling his nostrils. Her heat touching him, making promises. "Okay. I stand corrected."

"Why did you say that?"

"Let it go. I said I was wrong."

She moved back, but he held on to her hand. "There had to be a reason you brought it up."

He sighed. "Okay, it's your clothes."

She looked down at the baggy shorts. "What about them?"

"Here in Oroville, you seem to wear clothes that won't call attention to yourself. Is that the way you normally dress?" he asked, noting the defensiveness in her eyes. "Or was the kind of stuff you wore at Club Nirvana the real you?"

"How ridiculous." She shook away from him, grabbed the pitcher of iced tea and topped up her glass. Then she added a lot of sugar. "I was on vacation. On a tropical island. Of course I dressed differently."

"See? I told you I was wrong." It wasn't so much the clothes but her demeanor that had him wondering. "Are we going for that swim before it gets too dark?"

She frowned, glancing out the window.

"Or maybe we could go to town," he suggested. "Catch a movie."

Her frown deepened as she seemed to consider her options.

"Nobody will be at the lake. I can still be your dirty little secret."

Surprise flickered in her eyes, and then wariness. "Very funny."

He kept his mouth shut. He shouldn't have teased her.

"Go get your swim trunks." She glanced at her watch. "Be out back in five minutes or you can go by yourself."

THE EVENING couldn't have been more perfect. A light breeze kept the air from being too warm or muggy. Just enough light showed them the way to Carly's favorite swimming hole. She hadn't been there since she'd returned to Oroville. Kind of nice that she'd share her first time back with Rick.

He stayed right beside her during the short hike into the woods, neither of them speaking, just enjoying the peace and quiet, the occasional squawking of disgruntled magpies.

Rick breathed in deeply. When he finally exhaled, the sound of contentment made Carly smile. "This place is awesome," he said, stopping to examine a particularly interesting quaking aspen bark that had become so weathered it looked as if it had been constructed of shingles.

She smiled. "It hasn't changed."

"That's what I mean. It's still untouched."

She cocked her head to the side, studying the way nature had made use of fallen trees, how many different shades of green there were in the colors of the leaves. She truly loved it here. City lights could never take the place of this natural beauty.

"Left or right? I can't remember."

The sound of Rick's voice broke into her musings and she automatically led him down the left fork to the lake. With the trees blocking out any remaining light, it was darker than she'd anticipated, the path a little trickier to maneuver.

She looked over her shoulder to see how Rick was keeping up. He followed not two feet behind her, his gaze trained on her legs. Safer that way, she knew, but she faltered anyway. He caught her when she stumbled.

He held her against his chest and whispered, "I'm fine back here. You pay attention to the path."

She nodded and straightened. But he didn't let her go, and instead crossed his arms in front of her, bringing her back against his chest, and then kissed the side of her neck.

She sighed. "Rick, we shouldn't."

"No one's around."

"It's not that."

"What then?"

Hard to concentrate when he kissed the back of her ear and then drew her earlobe between his teeth. He touched the fleshy lobe with his tongue, and she sagged against him, closing her eyes. His hands rested on her ribcage, a scant inch away from her breasts. Her desperate urge to shift and have him touch her nipples frightened her. They weren't on vacation anymore. This was Oroville….

With his tongue he flicked her lobe again, and then whispered, "I want to do that to you all over."

Her breath caught.

His hand moved down her belly to the juncture of her thighs. "Here."

She moaned, knowing she should stop him.

He stroked her through her shorts and continued to nip her lobe. His erection pressed against her backside. She moved her hips a little and he groaned in her ear.

"Come on," she said, using every ounce of willpower she possessed to shift away. "It's going to be pitch-black soon and all I have is this little pencil flashlight."

"Wait."

He pulled her back, and cupping her face with his hands, he kissed her on the mouth. No tongue. Just a determined kiss, a coaxing kiss that missed not a speck of her lips. Even when she parted her mouth he concentrated on nibbling and licking and sucking her lips until she was ready to sink to the grass.

He finally moved away, and said, "Okay, Livingston, lead on."

She swallowed, praying her voice still worked. "Maybe we should turn back."

"Chicken."

"You are so right."

He laughed. "Okay, I'll make you a deal. No touching. For the rest of the night." As if surrendering, he held up his hands. "I'll keep these to myself." He paused, and she could hear the smile in his voice when he added, "Unless you initiate the contact."

"Ha."

"As they say, darlin', the ball's in your court."

"Fine." She really would have appreciated hearing a little more conviction in her own voice. "Good."

She made an about-face and headed toward the creek, her awareness of him directly behind her even more heightened. What a snake. As if she didn't know his so-called deal was all part of the game to wear her down. Force her to make a move.

Her thoughts were doing back flips, bouncing between disappointment and annoyance. No doubt he expected her to cave in. Well, she was made of stronger stuff than that.

She hoped.

In a few minutes they got to the lake. Rick hadn't said a another word, and Carly was too stubborn to say anything either.

Even to remind him that it got muddy and slippery close to the water. He'd been here many times before. He should know to be cautious.

The thought barely gone, her foot hit a slick patch of earth and she slid down the bank. She managed to break her fall by hitting the ground with both hands, her butt prominently stuck in the air.

She heard Rick's muffled laughter and muttered a pithy word that would have shocked him if he'd heard it.

"Um, would you like some help up?" His voice shook with restrained laughter. "You'd have to give me the go-ahead first."

"No, thank you." Using her body's momentum, she pushed backwards and managed to stand upright. Icky, disgusting brown mud squished between her fingers.

Rick choked back a laugh and the temptation to rub her hands over his face and clean shirt nearly won out.

Seizing her last shred of control, she gingerly made her way to the edge of the water, crouched, and rinsed off her hands.

"I was going to remind you about how slippery it gets, but I figured you knew better than I did." He tried to hand her his towel.

Ignoring him, she pulled the one she'd brought from around her neck and dried her hands.

"You're not giving me the silent treatment. That wasn't my fault."

She smiled. "Of course not."

He gave her a skeptical look. "You're acting weird."

"Am I?" She found a dry spot near an aspen and stowed her towel.

In the daylight he was gorgeous enough, but with the rapidly dwindling twilight, he made her mouth water. Something about the way the shadows danced across his face gave him a roguish look that inspired all kinds of wicked thoughts. The kind of fantasies no one in Oroville would believe Pastor Ray's daughter capable of.

"Okay," he said finally, his tone baiting and full of cynicism. "Have it your way."

She gave him a smile that said she wasn't biting. "You want to go in first, or do you want me to?"

He grabbed the hem of his shirt and pulled it over his head. "Is that a trick question?"

At the sight of his rounded pecs and well-defined stomach muscles, she swallowed hard. Fought the urge to squeeze her legs together. Squelched the reflexive desire to tear off his shorts.

God, what was wrong with her? She knew better. In a way, this was still vacation for Rick. Not for her, though. This was real life. One that didn't include him.

"How is it on planet Carly?"

She blinked. "What?"

"Where have you been?"

"I, uh, I was just thinking about an upcoming deadline I have at school." She looked away. "Nothing important."

"Gee, thanks."

"What?"

"My company is so stimulating that you're thinking about work deadlines?"

She laughed, the sound rusty to her own ears. If he only knew... "Promise it won't happen again."

"Too late. My ego is irreversibly damaged." He unzipped his shorts.

"Right." She snorted, trying not to watch him finish undressing. "I don't think that's possible."

"What's that supposed to mean?"

"Don't be so touchy." She turned around. "I was only kidding—"

He'd taken off his shorts. He didn't have on swim trunks.

"Good God, Rick. Where's your bathing suit?"

"You don't need one to skinny-dip."

"We're not skinny-dipping. We agreed to go swimming. Two very different things."

He started laughing. "It's not like you haven't seen it all before."

She should look away. She couldn't. Especially since he was getting hard and her knees were getting weak.

"Do you want me to put my shorts back on? Or my boxers?"

"Did you even bring swim trunks?" She already knew the answer. All he had was a towel. And his bare chest.

She promptly lifted her gaze to his before she ended up attacking him and embarrassing herself.

"No. I didn't pack one. I never expected to go swimming here."

"You tried to trick me."

"What are you talking about?"

She put a hand on her hip. Indignation worked much better than temptation. "You pretended to go home and change."

"Oh." He rubbed his jaw. "Well, you see..."

"Don't try to deny it."

"This is ridiculous." He started to slip his shorts back on, hopping on one leg, having obvious difficulty staying balanced.

He was right. This whole conversation was absurd, but it sure beat thinking about how good he looked. How tempting it was to say the heck with propriety. "Well, don't get all huffy."

"You started this."

She pressed her lips together and then burst out laughing. "Gee, this sounds familiar."

He frowned at her, and then a grin lifted his lips. "We may look grown up..."

"Appearances really are deceiving." She tried not to watch him struggle with his shorts. That he hadn't fallen and slid into the lake by now was pretty amazing. Of course it would be good for a laugh. Not to mention cooling down the heat growing in her belly.

"I'll try not to take that remark personally."

"Oh, no, go right ahead."

"Cute." He muttered a curse when his foot missed the leg hole.

"Why was it so much easier taking those off?"

"I'm flattered you noticed."

"Brother." Why did she bother? He always managed to get the last word in. "Do you need help?"

"Sure." He looked up, his expression lit with interest.

"I meant that you could use my shoulder."

"You have other parts I'd rather use."

She laughed and shook her head, busying herself with storing her flashlight safely behind her towel. "Quit fooling around or it'll be time to go back."

"I don't have a curfew. Do you?"

At his serious tone, she looked at him. He'd stopped trying to get into his shorts.

In fact, he'd yanked them off entirely, and stood naked again.

12

SHE TOOK a deep breath. "I guess it's all right. I doubt anyone will show up here this late."

Although it wasn't anyone else that worried her. *She* was the problem. And her nearly irresistible urge to lie down right here. But then reason returned, and she turned away. Not in an obvious way. Casually. As if he stripped in front of her every day. Which he had on the island. Oh, God...

Pretending disinterest, she peeled off her own clothes until she got to the bikini she'd bought at Club Nirvana's gift shop.

She'd had to dig it out of her bottom drawer where she kept mismatched socks and emergency underwear. The stretched-out kind that she wore only if she had nothing else clean. Why she didn't wear her more modest suit, the one she'd be comfortable wearing at the Fourth of July town picnic she didn't know.

That was a lie. She knew darn well why she'd chosen to wear the skimpy bikini. God, had she evolved into one of those pathetic girls who said no but meant yes?

She heard a splash just as she pulled off her shorts and laid them on the towel along with her shirt.

"Damn, but it's cold." He coughed. "I mean, the water's great. Come on in."

Carly laughed. "You must be getting old. It's no colder than it was the two summers you were here. Of course, you were wearing swim trunks then."

"Yeah, that made a difference."

She could barely see his head and shoulders surfacing the water. It had suddenly gotten so dark it seemed as if someone had turned off the lights. The only illumination came from the moon, which shone between the trees. The beams hit the water like iridescent ribbons.

"Are you coming in or not?"

She grinned at his impatience. "I don't know. Found any creepy-crawly things yet?"

"Damn it, Carly." His head bobbed and he appeared to be moving toward the bank.

"Look who's chicken now." She hurried to the edge of the water and slowly eased in. It really wasn't cold and she easily submerged to her waist. "Rick?"

A splash sounded behind her. She spun around. Nothing.

And then she felt something wrap around her legs. She covered her mouth to keep from screaming.

Suddenly he popped out of the water, saying, "Rick to the rescue." Surprised, she nearly toppled backward.

She slapped at his shoulders. "You moron."

"What?" Laughing, he grabbed her by the waist. "I was saving you from the creepy-crawlies."

"Okay, I deserved that one. Now we're even."

"Think so?" He slid an arm around her, and she went boneless, letting him guide her toward him.

"The water isn't cold," she murmured, relishing the way it soothed her fevered skin. "It feels great."

Suddenly he released her and moved back nearly a yard. "Shit, I'm sorry. I promised no touching."

She bit her lip before she said something she'd regret. Before she strangled him. "That's right. You did." With a lift of her chin she laid back in the water and backstroked away from him.

"It's not very deep in that direction."

"I know."

"It's dark. We should stick close together."

"Ha."

"I'm serious."

"You *are* getting old."

He grunted. "Getting wiser, I like to think. You're headed right for a fallen tree trunk."

She knew exactly where he meant. The tree had been downed by a thunderstorm six years ago. She kept swimming backwards another couple of yards and then stopped just short of the tree. She planted her feet on the bottom and stood, smoothing her wet hair back.

"Do you want me to feel totally useless?" He swam up to her but stopped within arm's length. "You could have at least pretended you didn't know about the tree."

"Ah, you want us to play Damsel in Distress and Knight in Shining Armor."

"Trust me. You don't know what I want us to play."

Her breath caught at the way his voice lowered, how husky it sounded. "Tell me," she whispered.

He remained silent for a moment. "You don't want to go there, Carly."

"You brought it up." Dangerous talk. She shivered with anticipation.

"Or maybe you do want it." He moved a little closer. "Maybe some of the barriers are coming down."

She'd asked for this. "Maybe."

"It's up to you."

She swallowed. This wasn't vacation. This was reality and as much as she wanted to play the game, she didn't want to face the consequences.

"Carly?"

"I'm thinking."

He laughed. She did, too. It was so easy to be with him, to be able to act naturally and not worry. That was the growing problem. She could fall for him. Too easily.

"Why don't you come over here and think?" He held out his arms. Not overtly. He kind of just let them float on top of the water.

She moved toward him, letting the water's resistance slow her down, leaving room for second thoughts. None came. She wanted desperately to feel his skin against hers, to kiss him, to have him kiss her back. Hard, and then gently the way he had before.

When she stopped right in front of him, he didn't hesitate. No baiting. No smugness. He simply put his hands on her waist and drew her closer, and then claimed her mouth.

She slid her arms around his neck and savored the feel of his bare chest pressed to her breasts. He molded his hands to the small of her back, down the curve of her backside and drew her against him. His erection prodded her belly. Gave her goose bumps. Made her knees weak. Reduced her resolve to a farce.

He moaned from deep in his throat, and plunged his tongue into her mouth. She gave as good as she got, and when he undid the back strings of her bikini bra she didn't protest. He lifted the fabric above her breasts and cupped both his palms over her nipples.

She shivered with the delicious sensation.

He drew back to look at her. "Cold?"

She shook her head.

"You okay?"

She nodded.

He laughed softly. "Cat got your tongue?"

Carly shivered again, the friction caused by his palms against her nipples so seductive she wanted to force his mouth to her breasts. "You want to waste time talking?"

He let out a low groan, and as if he'd read her mind, lowered his mouth to taste her. He flicked his tongue over the protruding bud and then lightly clamped his teeth around it while continuing to tease her with his tongue.

She shifted and he suckled harder, taking as much of her as he could into his mouth. He slid his hand beneath her bikini bottom and kneaded her flesh. Arching her neck, her back, she gave him complete access. But when he tried to pull off her bottoms, she tensed.

He moved his hand away, but kept suckling her, and she tried to relax. But the crazy thoughts started coming again, filling her head with doubt and fear.

Finally, he brought up his head and lightly kissed her on the lips. "What's wrong?"

"Nothing."

"Sure."

"Nothing I can really explain." She couldn't see his face. The moon was behind him. Unfortunately he could probably see hers. She tried to look away. He guided her face back to his.

He kissed her gently. "I like you. A lot. Always have. And I won't make any promises I can't keep."

"I know. And I'm not asking for any."

She let her hand slide from his shoulder down his chest, liking the feel of nicely curved muscle under her palm. His nipple stuck out and she liked the feel of it, too.

"Careful," he whispered, his chest expanding under her touch. "You're making me crazy."

"This wasn't supposed to happen," she whispered back.

He went still. "Is that what you want? To pretend nothing has changed, that we didn't have the most incredible week of our entire lives?" He chuckled softly. "Or at least from my perspective."

Pleasure filled every pore of her being. "Mine, too."

He combed a hand through her hair. "What are we going to do about it?"

She sighed.

He cupped her breast and bent his head to suck hard

on her nipple again. He came up to add, "I'm a patient man, Carly. Sooner or later you'll come around, and I'll be here."

"Confident, aren't—?" She gasped when he pulled her against him and his erection slid up her belly.

He slanted his mouth over hers, kissing her hard, purposefully, and she clung to him, wanting to touch him lower, to wrap her hand around his silky thickness.

His tongue invaded her mouth, robbed her of breath, made her boneless and accomplished its mission. Spelled out what she was missing. He ran his palms down her hips, over her thighs and then back up to cup her breasts.

She needed no more urging. She leaned into him, freely, eagerly, offering him a response she'd thought she was too cautious to give. When he finally broke the kiss to touch his tongue to her nipple, she let one hand follow his lead, molding his right hip.

She stopped there and splayed her hand toward his penis. She grasped him and he jerked, shuddering, the vibration in his chest resonating throughout her body.

He groaned against her breast, and then came up and kissed her on the mouth, hard, fast. "I said I was patient," he whispered as he took her by the wrist and moved her hand away. "Not a damn saint."

Then he brought her hand to his lips, kissed her palm, and pulled her to shore.

"DID YOU SEE the way she was carrying on with that man? Shameful, I tell you," Mildred Taylor said to Thelma Wilson. "Does the girl have no sense of decorum? I know her mama and daddy brought her up better than that.''

''Decorum? What kind of word is that?'' Thelma peered dubiously at her blue-gray hair in the mirror.

Carly froze outside the bathroom door where she'd just come from putting on a smock, and debated between slipping back inside or trying to edge her way out the door of Vivian's Beauty World. She knew this would happen. The whole town knew about her and Rick by now.

Had her father heard? Had some well-meaning soul slipped him a note, or whispered in his ear about how his daughter was an embarrassment to him and his congregation?

''Don't you ever watch 'Oprah'?'' Mildred asked, her back to Carly as she rearranged the chair cushion under the hairdryer.

''I'm not sure about this style,'' Thelma leaned closer to the mirror. ''Vivian talked me into it. Do you think it's too short?''

''It's not too short, you old fool, it's too blue.'' Mildred squeezed her wide hips in between the armrests and adjusted the dryer over her headful of tiny curlers. ''Anyway, as I was saying...''

Carly took a step back toward the bathroom.

Thelma turned from the mirror to glare at Mildred. Her eyes lit up when she saw Carly. ''Well, hello there, honey. I heard you were back in town.''

Carly smiled feebly.

Mildred struggled to sit up straight and then pushed the dryer out of the way. ''My goodness, Carly Saunders, I swear you've grown three inches.''

Carly hadn't grown a smidgen since the tenth grade, but she wasn't about to argue with the town's biggest busybody. "Hello, Mrs. Taylor, Mrs. Wilson, nice to see you both."

"I knew you'd come back." Mrs. Taylor nodded approvingly. Certainly not the reception Carly had expected after what she'd overheard. "Some of the others, like Harriet and Gerdie, told me I was crazy. A bright girl like you wouldn't come back. You could get a job anywhere. Sure you could, I told them, but you'd be back nonetheless. You're our kind. Not like that shameless hussy Belinda Myers."

"Hush, Mildred." Thelma Wilson gave the other woman a reproving look. "Carly and Belinda are friends. They went to school together."

Mrs. Taylor lifted her chin, the wattle that two generations of kids had privately laughed about more pronounced than Carly remembered. "I'm not saying anything about Belinda that she hasn't advertised for everyone to see. Parading around with that man like she's doing. If she were my daughter I'd have her locked in her room by now."

They'd been talking about Belinda.

Relief swamped Carly. She sank into the nearest chair to wait for Missy, Vivian's daughter who'd joined in her mother's business. Being more willing to experiment with contemporary styles and shades, Missy cut and colored most of Oroville's younger population.

"Locked in her room." Thelma snorted with derision. "She's a grown woman. Old enough to decide who she wants to run around with. I swear, you are getting nosier and grumpier in your golden years.''

"At least my hair isn't blue." Mrs. Taylor jammed the plastic bubble of the hair dryer back over her head and yanked a magazine off the table beside her.

"Good. Bury your nose in that instead of other folks' business." Thelma gave her hair a final pat, left a couple of dollar bills at Vivian's work station and smiled at Carly. "Nice to see you back."

She walked out of the shop leaving a trail of lavender scent Carly remembered from as far back as her first trip to Wilson's bakery with her mother over twenty years ago. Mr. Wilson had still been alive and they'd run the bakery together. He'd slip Carly a cookie and Mrs. Wilson would scold him. But when no one was looking she'd do the same.

They'd both loved children, but had never had any of their own. That's probably why they spoiled everyone else's. Everyone for fifty miles knew the loving couple, and when Mr. Wilson had passed away from cancer five years ago, the memorial service had been standing room only.

That was the thing about a small town. Even though everyone knew everyone else's business, there was also a lot of caring and kinship that couldn't be found anywhere else. Carly felt that she belonged here, that she was an integral part of the community.

Rick didn't understand. He'd led a nomadic, adventurous life. It was in his blood. Belonging meant nothing....

Darn it. Why did she have to start thinking about him now? Flashbacks from last night at the lake made her skin tingle, her heart race. Thinking about how his hard, heavy erection had stroked her belly, mimicking the ultimate act…

A loud squeak made her start.

"Hey, you." Missy had entered the beauty shop through the back door, a milkshake from Libby's Diner in her hand. "Hope you haven't been waiting long. I told Mama to mark me off for a full hour lunch break."

"No problem. I've just been catching up with everyone." Carly stared at Missy's long red nails. They had little gold stars painted on the tips.

"Oh, God, poor you." Missy darted a disdainful look at Mildred Taylor. "I guess I just blew my tip."

Carly laughed. "It's okay. Really."

Missy rolled her dramatically made-up eyes, fringed with false eyelashes. She truly was one of Oroville's oddballs. Even in high school, two years ahead of Carly, she'd been a rebel. Someone who'd stood out. Someone about whom all the mothers had warned their sons. Missy was the first person Carly would have bet would leave Oroville and never look back.

Yet curiously, after a year in Las Vegas, she'd returned to work in her mother's beauty parlor. Lucky for Carly, anyway, since Missy was a whiz with scissors. In fact, she'd been starting to pick up clients from as far as Cedar City and it wasn't easy to get a last-minute appointment anymore.

Missy got up close to the mirror and checked her teeth. Then she stepped back, patted her newly platinum-blond hair and said, "You just want a trim, I suppose."

"That's it." Carly stared at herself in the mirror. Her hair looked dark after being back from the Caribbean for only three weeks. "And a few highlights around the face if you have time."

"No problemo." Missy got out a color chart, and then studied Carly's hair. "You wanna go lighter?"

"You mean overall?"

Missy shrugged. "I was thinking the highlights, but a new color altogether would be cool."

Carly's thoughts immediately went to Rick. Would he think the change was for his benefit? Of course he would, and he'd be right. Darn it. "I'll stick with highlights."

As Missy got out the ingredients, she said, "Tell me about your big adventure. And don't you dare leave out a single juicy detail."

Carly winced, wondering what Missy was getting at. "Nothing to tell."

"That's not what I heard."

No one knew about Club Nirvana. Of course her parents knew she'd been on vacation in the Caribbean, but she hadn't said much about it. Just that she'd had a great time. "I don't know who you've been talking to but—"

Missy bent close to her ear. "Look, I've been stuck here for the past six years while you've been living it up in Salt Lake City. I wanna hear it all. Damn it."

Carly choked back a laugh. Missy hadn't been referring to her Caribbean trip at all. Never underestimate a guilty conscience. It would do her in yet. "Going to school isn't what I call living it up."

Missy shook out a plastic cape and secured it

around Carly's neck. "Don't tell me you didn't use the opportunity to cat around, with no daddy looking down from the pulpit and no Mildred Taylor talking over the backyard fence." She got down close to Carly's ear again. "You're not the Little Miss Innocent everyone thinks, and it's not like I'm gonna blab any stories you tell me. You know me better than that."

Carly darted a look around. Mrs. Taylor couldn't hear anything under the dryer, and Vivian was still up front on the phone. "Why on earth would you say that?"

"Don't get all defensive. I only mean that everyone around here thinks you're the model daughter, the perfect student. I bet every girl in this town at one time or another was asked by her parents why she couldn't be more like Carly Saunders."

"That's ridiculous."

"I'm telling you." She gave an emphatic nod, and grabbed the scissors. "Not that I care. I'm just saying that's the way it is, only I know you're not as squeaky clean as they all think."

Carly grinned. "Did I ever pretend to be squeaky clean?"

"Good point. Anyway, not that I have proof," Missy said with a taunting curve of her lips, "but I swear you were the last one out of Mr. Wigg's biology class the day all the frogs were liberated."

Carly burst out laughing. Even Vivian glanced over her shoulder. "I had nothing to do with that."

"Of course not. Not you." Still smiling, Missy

picked up a lock of Carly's hair and frowned. "When was the last time you had a trim?"

"About five weeks ago." Carly relaxed now that she knew Missy wasn't referring to anything more than the poor frogs that had been destined to be dissected the next day. "I have a question for you."

"Ha. You won't give me any juicy tidbits and I'm supposed to answer you." Missy lifted her chin in a snub, but couldn't keep a straight face. "What?"

"Why did you come back?"

Missy shrugged a shoulder. "Las Vegas wasn't all it was cracked up to be." A self-mocking grin curved her lips. "Besides, here in Oroville I'm the best damn hair stylist north of Cedar City. In Vegas there were so many really good transplanted L.A. hairdressers it was hard to build a decent clientele."

"It isn't so bad being back, is it?"

"Nah. You know me...I like the attention. In a place like Las Vegas everybody's as weird as me. I never got a second look."

Carly smiled. Missy got major points for being honest.

Missy studied the color chart again and brought a sample shade up to Carly's hair. She made a face, discarded it and tried another. "Mind if I try mixing a couple of colors? I think a gold and auburn combination would look awesome."

"Go for it."

Missy really was a good hairdresser, in Carly's opinion, and gifted with smarts and personality. Finding a job and building a clientele in any city wouldn't be a problem. They were all lucky to have her back.

If only because she wanted to be a big fish in a small pond.

Missy squirted something out of a tube into a bowl. "So back to you. What's the dirt?"

Carly frowned at the deep burgundy shade, starting to have second thoughts about this two-tone color deal. "Sorry to disappoint you—"

The bell over the front door rang as it opened.

Missy looked up and stopped. "Well, color me happy. Look at that amazing hunk of man that just walked in."

Carly cringed, knowing who it was before she looked in the mirror to see behind her. Rick's amused eyes met hers for an instant.

"Hey, Carly," he said and made himself at home in the chair beside her. "So this is where you've been hiding from me."

13
_____

"MIND IF I sit here?" Rick asked the blonde in the tight pink sweater. If her breasts were real, he'd eat his new Harley. He made a point of looking her in the eyes.

"Suit yourself." She glanced over at Carly, who went from glaring to looking as if she were going to jump out of the chair, and then the hairdresser looked back at him. "Who are you?"

The way she wrinkled her nose and cocked her head to the side sparked his memory. He remembered her from the lake that last summer he'd spent at Gram's. Not her name, but, damn, he hoped the Harley would go down easier with salt.

He leaned back in the chair and smiled. "I'm crushed you don't remember."

Her frown deepened and her gaze went back to Carly.

An older plump woman with knee-high hose that stopped short of her dress hem sat under a dryer, the magazine she'd been reading forgotten as she stared at him.

"Hi." He winked, but she didn't respond. Not a word. Not even a blink of an eye.

"This is Rick," Carly finally said, her tone and expression not one bit pleased. "Agatha Weaver's grandson."

The blonde's eyes widened. "Oh, my God. I remember you now. You're the boy who—" She stopped and glanced impishly at the woman at the front desk who'd already looked him over. "Yeah, I remember you." She gave him an obvious once-over. "Well, didn't you just turn out fine?"

He smiled. "You're looking pretty good yourself."

Carly frowned at them both. Thank God the blonde hadn't spilled the beans about that day by the lake. It was a long time ago, and he'd been just a hormonal kid, but still… Damn, he wished he could remember her name.

"Excuse me, Missy." The lady behind the desk called out. "Can you do another shampoo and set this afternoon?"

Missy. That was it.

Missy rolled her eyes. "Damn old farts," she muttered. "I can do the same thing faster with a curling iron but nooo, they all want curlers in their hair." Louder she said, "Sorry, Mom, not today."

Rick chuckled, and then caught the murderous glint in Carly's eyes. "What?"

"Don't you have something to do?" she asked, not even trying to hide her annoyance.

"Yeah."

"Something *else* to do?" She gave him a meaningful look he chose to ignore.

Out of the corner of his eye, he noticed the curious look Missy was giving them and he winked at Carly.

"Sorry, honey, I forgot you don't like to be seen with me in public."

She blushed, her eyes flashing furiously. "You jerk."

Laughing, Missy elbowed Carly's shoulder. "And you said there was nothing to tell."

"There isn't," Carly said tightly, clearly finding no humor in the situation.

Suffering a twinge of conscience, Rick sighed. "Unfortunately, she's right."

"Uh-huh." Missy's knowing smile as she stirred some stuff in a bowl increased his regret.

"Not for lack of trying, I will admit."

Missy gave Carly a look of disbelief that would have ordinarily stroked his ego—if he didn't feel like such a jerk. "Feel free to pawn him off on me."

He glanced at his watch. "All kidding aside, how long are you gonna be?"

"Why?"

Fascinated, he watched Missy section off Carly's hair and start painting quarter inch strips of a deep red. "I was just having coffee with your mom. She told me you were here, and, since I had to come to town anyway, I figured we could have lunch when you're done."

Carly darted him a panicked look. "You had coffee with my mom?"

He frowned at Missy. "Are you making her hair red?"

"No, I'm highlighting it."

"But that's red paint."

Missy laughed. "It's not paint nor is it red."

"Where did you have coffee with my mother?" Carly asked, impatience clipping her voice.

"At your house. I was looking for you, and she invited me in." He continued to watch Missy pile on the god-awful color. "That looks red to me."

"Not that it's any of your business." Carly gave him a warning look. "Don't pay any attention to him, Missy."

Brave words except he could see Carly checking out the color with trepidation, her anxious gaze darting from the brush Missy dipped into the bowl to the streaks she painted in Carly's hair.

He sure hoped Missy knew what she was doing. "What time shall I come back for you?"

"For what?"

"Lunch."

"I'm busy this afternoon."

"No, you aren't."

She turned to give him an arch look.

Missy scowled. "Don't turn your head."

"Sorry." Carly obediently looked straight ahead into the mirror, caught Rick's reflection and made a face. "I have an appointment this afternoon with—"

"No, she cancelled."

"Who?"

"Mrs. Sizemore, your principal."

Carly's mouth parted as she stared in confusion.

"Your mom told me she phoned right after you left." He stood and checked out his hair in the mirror. It definitely needed a trim. "She needs to reschedule. See? You are free for lunch."

"And you're assuming I'd like to spend it with you," she said dryly.

Missy hooted with laughter.

"That's my girl." He grinned. "She loves playing hard to get."

Carly waved a dismissive hand. "He's just as annoying as he was when he was fifteen. Some guys never grow up."

Her nonchalance didn't fool him. Both anger and anxiety showed in her expressive face. He was so damn tempted to remind her that she hadn't been annoyed last night when he'd suckled her breasts, and explored the inside of her mouth with his tongue.

Of course he wouldn't. It was just a brief fantasy. But her attitude was really starting to piss him off. It wasn't as if he was some undesirable she should be ashamed of.

He'd let her have her way. For now.

Abruptly he stood. Took another look in the mirror. "I need a trim myself," he said to Missy. "You have some time this week?"

"I'm pretty booked, but if you come tomorrow morning at eight-thirty I can do you before my first appointment."

"I'll be here."

"Or better yet. How about this evening after my last cut?" Missy smiled. "Maybe after, we can have a drink. A new country-and-western bar opened in Cedar City last week."

Carly stiffened, subtly enough, and her expression remained impassive, but there'd been enough of a reaction that Missy suddenly darted her an uncertain look.

Missy put down the hair-color stuff. "Is that okay with you, Carly?"

"Why are you asking me?" Carly asked with a huff. "I'm not his baby-sitter."

"I don't want to step on any toes."

Carly snorted. "You're not. Can we get back to my hair before you have gray to cover, too?"

Chuckling, Missy went back to her paint job. She smiled at Rick. "Come by around six, okay?"

"Six it is."

Carly wouldn't even look at him. He watched her glare at the woman under the dryer trying desperately to hear what was going on, and then she looked straight ahead, scowling at herself in the mirror. Her obvious display of jealousy pleased the hell out of him.

Without saying anything to her, he left the beauty shop whistling.

CARLY LOOKED OUT her window toward Rick's house. No lights were on. Nine o'clock. He was probably still out with Missy. Not that Carly cared. Okay, so she did a little. Maybe more than a little.

Which was incredibly stupid. She should be grateful Missy had taken him off her hands. Let them parade around town and get stared at, discussed behind their backs. Missy didn't care about public opinion, nor did she have to, and when Rick left town Missy would find another distraction. Or maybe they'd hit it off well enough that they'd meet on vacations twice a year or maybe she'd even move to L.A.

The thought should have cheered Carly. It depressed the heck out of her.

She sat on the window seat and stared out into the darkness. If Rick asked her to move to L.A. with him, would she do it? Could she? The thought of spending the rest of her life in a city like L.A. depressed her even more. But then she might never see Rick again.

Darn it. Why had she ever gone to Club Nirvana? Why did she have to see Rick again after all those years? Why did she have to give in to temptation with him?

The phone rang and, tempted as she was to ignore it, her parents weren't home and it could be them. They really needed to invest in caller ID.

She grabbed the cordless off her nightstand and returned to the window seat before hitting Talk.

"Carly?" It was Ginger, her small distraught voice inspiring a wave of guilt.

"Hi. What's going on?"

"Have you called him?"

"Rick's here."

"In Oroville?"

"Yes."

"Is Tony with him?" Excitement elevated her voice.

Carly shook her head. She wished Ginger could see and hear herself. This wasn't like her. This whole transformation was so pathetic. "No."

"Oh. I guess he wouldn't be." Ginger sighed. "I am so jealous."

"Why?"

"Are you kidding? I knew he'd go see you. I knew it from the first day that this was going to be something big."

Carly tapped down the giddy excitement buzzing in her head. "He's not here to see me."

"Why else would he be there?"

"To sell his grandmother's house."

After a brief silence, Ginger chuckled. "Right. Okay, so what did he say about Tony?"

Carly groaned to herself. Whoever had said confession was good for the soul? "We haven't really discussed anything like that."

"What do you mean? Hasn't he even mentioned Tony? Or me? Or anything about us?"

"I haven't had the opportunity to bring you up." Carly bit her lip at the long silence that followed. "The thing is, he just got here."

"Have you talked to him at all?"

"Well, yeah." She ought to come right out and tell Ginger the ugly truth—if Tony had been interested, he would have called by now. "To be honest, I wasn't happy to see him so I haven't exactly put out the welcome mat."

Ginger sniffed. "Doesn't that suck? I'm dying here, hoping Tony will call, and Rick shows up on your front door and you don't even want him."

Carly's first instinct was to protest. It wasn't that she didn't want him. Sadly, she feared wanting him too much. She feared ending up like Ginger, missing out on life, wanting a future that couldn't be, waiting around for a call that would never come. Wisely she kept her mouth shut.

"Tell you what," she said finally. "I promise to talk to him but—"

"When?"

"Let me finish. I have a condition."

"Anything."

"Whatever he has to say I'll pass it on, even if it sucks the big one, no sugar coating, but then we drop it."

"Of course," Ginger said eagerly.

"I'm serious, Ginger. I don't want to be mean—"

A light came on next door. Downstairs, inside the front door. And then another in the kitchen.

"I said okay," Ginger snapped, and then murmured, "Sorry, I know you're trying to help. When will you talk to him?"

"Tomorrow." She moved the curtain a fraction to get a better look.

"For sure?"

"Yes."

"In the morning?"

"Ginger!"

"I just wanted to make sure I was home when you called. That's all. Jeez."

Carly briefly closed her eyes. Why did intelligent, sensible women become moronic over men? She'd known Ginger since sophomore year at university and one of the things that had impressed her was Ginger's ambition and focus.

She'd known she wanted to be a special-ed teacher since she was in the seventh grade and she'd allowed no distractions, nothing that would derail her studies. But since she'd returned from vacation, she hadn't once mentioned her new job. Every call had been about Tony.

"What's going on at school?" Carly asked.

"School?"

"As in your job?"

"Oh, that school. We start in less than two weeks."

"I assume your lesson plans have been approved and all that good stuff."

Ginger hesitated. "I'll be turning them in tomorrow."

"I thought they were due—"

"No lectures, okay?"

"Fine." She hadn't planned on delivering one.

A light coming on in Rick's bedroom upstairs caught her attention. At least, it was the same room he'd used as a boy.

"Look, Carly, I appreciate what you're doing for me by talking to Rick, and I'm well aware I'm being a total lunatic. But this is it. I promise."

"I'm glad you at least know you're nuts."

Ginger laughed softly. "Small consolation."

"Look, I've gotta go," Carly said, cradling the phone while she pulled on her tennis shoes. "I'll call *in the morning,* okay?"

"You're the absolute best."

"Right."

"Carly, wait. Don't blow it with Rick. He's one of the good ones."

Carly bit her lip and hung up. What did Ginger know? Look where caring too much had gotten *her.*

Mentally kicking herself, she decided she'd go over there right now. Before her parents got home. Talk to Rick about Ginger and Tony, as useless as that would be. But at least she'd get it over with. And then if he wanted to spend the rest of his time here with Missy, then God bless him. She wouldn't have to see him again the rest of his visit.

She checked her hair in the mirror. The highlights had turned out really well. A mixture of gold and auburn framed her face and brightened her complexion. The cut was good, too, slightly more contemporary than her last one.

She ran a quick brush through her hair and then used a little gel to keep one side from sticking up. She added a touch of blush to her cheeks and clear gloss to her lips but that was it. She didn't want him to think she was doing any of this for his benefit.

She shook her head at her own foolishness as she trotted down the stairs, stopping to look out the front window in case her parents were coming down the drive. They probably wouldn't be home for another hour or two, enough time for her to have a talk with Rick, come home and get to bed.

Tomorrow would be a busy day. She'd promised to help out at the school in the afternoon in preparation for classes starting soon.

She didn't bother locking the house as she slipped out the back door. Few people even had locks in Oroville. They were totally unnecessary. People trusted each other, and watched out for their neighbors. Another bonus of small-town living.

At the hedge that divided the two properties, Carly

looked up to make sure the light was still on. It was, and he'd opened the window. The blue floral curtain fluttered slightly in the gentle summer breeze.

And then she saw his silhouette as he pulled off his shirt. He hesitated near the window and she saw him clearly as he pushed a hand through his hair.

She told herself to look away. Reminded herself it was rude and immoral to watch, but she couldn't do it. She couldn't tear her gaze away from the breadth of his shoulders, the lean curve of muscle that defined his pecs, the arrow of brown hair that disappeared into the waistband of his jeans.

Instead she shrank back into the shadows and waited to see what he'd do next. For a moment he disappeared and then he came back to the window, bracing his hands on the sill as he leaned out.

He peered at her house, in the direction of her bedroom, she thought, a serious look on his face. She followed his gaze, curious as to what he saw. But there was nothing, really. The house was mostly dark except for the lamp they always left on in the living room, and the soft glow of the nightlight that burned in the upstairs hall.

He continued to stand there, the moonlight showing off his tanned chest and flat belly, and making her wonder if she had finally lost her mind. She had no business going over there at this time of night. Just watching him made her insides quiver, made dampness grow between her thighs.

She briefly closed her eyes, struggling for sanity. Tomorrow would be better. They could talk over coffee. Maybe meet at a coffee shop in Cedar City. The last thing she needed was to end up in the sack with him. This infatuation had to stop sometime….

He yawned and stretched and then disappeared again.

Panic swept her. Weird, inexplicable apprehension, as if she'd never see him again.

She quickly pushed her way through the hedges, ignoring the broken branch that scraped her leg and caught on her shorts. By the time she got to his door, the foyer light had been turned off.

She hesitated, uselessly telling herself once again how much better it would be to wait until morning. As if she would get any sleep. She needed to talk to him. Not just about Ginger, but about how he behaved around her in town.

He was reasonable, and she knew it wasn't his intention to embarrass her. He'd understand once she explained about the Mildred Taylors of Oroville, how easily his teasing could be misconstrued.

Who was she kidding? She had to see him. Period.

She made up her mind and knocked. The back door didn't have a doorbell, so after about a minute she knocked again. Another minute later, he opened the door.

Rick smiled. He hadn't bothered to put his shirt back on, or snap his jeans. "It wasn't locked."

"I'd never just walk in."

He shrugged and stepped back.

"I'm only going to be a moment," she said, gingerly crossing the threshold, and daring to let her gaze linger on his chest. "I know it's late."

"Your hair…it looks good."

She grinned at the surprise in his voice. "I trust Missy. She's a good hairdresser. Yours looks good, too, though she didn't take much off."

"Just a trim. That's all I wanted." He gestured toward the kitchen table. "Sit down."

"There's no need. I really won't be—"

"Carly. Sit."

"Okay, but just for a minute."

"Right." One side of his mouth lifted in a lopsided smile. But he looked tired. As if he'd had a long hard evening.

Jealousy tied a knot in her tummy. "How was that bar in Cedar City?"

"What?" He'd gone straight to the cabinet and got down two glasses.

"The one you went to with Missy tonight."

"I didn't go anywhere with Missy."

"But she asked earlier."

"So? That didn't mean I had to accept." He opened the refrigerator and studied the contents for a moment. "I don't have much. Wine, beer or water?"

"Nothing, thanks. I'm really not staying long."

He got out a bottle of white wine and poured some in each glass, and then put one on the table in front of her before sitting in the opposite chair.

"I would have preferred water."

"You had your chance." He tipped his glass up to his lips before setting it on the table.

"What's wrong?"

"What do you mean?"

"You're in a peculiar mood."

He shrugged. "Tired, I guess."

"Why? I mean, what did you do all day?"

He studied her for a moment, his expression so unreadable it was unnatural. "What do you care?"

Tensing, Carly picked up the wine and took a sip. He didn't look angry or anything, but he was being awfully short. He looked at her, his hazel eyes dark and brooding, and when she saw a flicker of hurt, she finally got it.

For all his teasing and taunting at Vivian's Beauty World, his feelings had been hurt. Oh, God, *she'd* hurt his feelings.

"Rick, I, uh, I—" She stood. "It's late. You're tired. I shouldn't have come. Tomorrow we'll talk."

She got three steps away when he grabbed her by the wrist and tugged her towards him.

"Don't go." He didn't hold too tightly, but firmly enough that she'd have to really yank away if she wanted to be free. When she didn't resist, he pulled her closer until she ended up on his lap.

"Rick." She tried to get up, but he put his arms around her. His skin was warm and musky-scented and she had the wildest urge to lie her cheek on his chest.

"Nobody is here watching," he murmured and pressed his lips to the side of her neck, working his way to the curve of her shoulder.

"That's what I wanted to talk to you about. One of the things, anyway." She gasped and closed her eyes when he moved back up to the tender spot behind her ear.

"So talk."

She smiled. "Like this?"

"Sure," he murmured against her skin.

"This isn't fair."

He gave a short humorless laugh. "I'm done with being fair."

"Rick." She jerked back to look at him. He'd been drinking, she realized. Not a lot, she didn't think, but more than the wine he'd sipped.

"What?" He slid a hand around her nape and guided her down to his mouth.

Their lips met gently. He teased hers apart with his tongue and then plunged inside. He tasted faintly of rum and lime, and a touch of the chardonnay.

His restless hand played with the hem of her shirt, the tips of his fingers brushing the bare skin of her belly. She didn't stop him when he slid his palm up toward her breast. But with a sudden start, she realized the curtains were open and they could be seen from the driveway if anyone came by.

Rick pulled back and followed her gaze to the window. And then his darkened gaze rested on her face. "Let's go upstairs," he whispered.

She hesitated, but only for a moment, and then got up and took his hand.

14

RICK HOPED Carly knew what she was doing. He sure as hell didn't. She wasn't the kind of woman you messed with, the kind who was happy with casual sex. Despite her quest for adventure at Club Nirvana, he knew this. If he had a half a brain, a shred of decency, he'd leave her the hell alone. His life was too screwed up right now to offer her anything. Assuming she'd even want him.

She had too much going for her to need or want anyone. Smart, confident, focused, roots in the community, surrounded by people who loved and respected her.

He grabbed the bottle of wine off the counter and took it with them as they held hands up the stairs. Thank God he'd washed the sheets this morning and picked up the two piles of dirty socks and grubby running shoes.

"You're using your old room," she said as they stood at the door.

"I thought about sleeping in Gram's bed since it's queen-size but I think that mattress dates back to the eighteen hundreds. I don't know how she could stand it."

Carly smiled. "The last five years she preferred sleeping on the downstairs recliner."

Guilt ambushed him. He'd had the time. He should have been here to help Gram, but he hadn't realized until it was too late how rapidly her health had declined. He'd been too self-absorbed, too concerned with making his mark in the world. His parents' world. What a waste of time.

Yet there was no admonishment in Carly's tone, nor in the gentle smile on her lips, in her eyes. She'd always seemed to understand him even though she was younger and less sophisticated. At least he wanted to believe she had.

"Frankly, I'm surprised this mattress is in any better shape," she said as they walked into the room. She pushed down on it with her hand. "I think everything in the house has pretty much been here for—" She laughed. "Since before I was born."

He smiled. "You have a great laugh."

She laughed again, this time more a short bark of disbelief.

"Great eyes. Great hair. Awesome lips." He put the wine on the nightstand along with his glass.

"Knock it off." A pretty pink crept into her cheeks and she turned away. "The floor looks good. Did you do something to it?"

"I stripped, sanded and revarnished it. I figured I'd experiment up here before I tackle downstairs, since, frankly, I wasn't sure what the hell I was doing."

"Really?" She looked back at him, eyebrows arched in surprise. "You'd never done this before?"

"Nah, I read one of those how-to books at the library last week."

"Wow!" She lifted the tan braided rug Agatha had made at least twenty years ago and inspected the hardwood floor more closely. "You did as good a job as Mr. Lamm did in our dining room and he does it for a living."

Pride swelled in his chest at the admiration in her eyes. Of course, she was probably only carrying on to distract him, so that he wouldn't jump her bones as he wanted to do more than anything.

She walked around the bed, running her palms up one of the maple posters. "Are you going to work your magic on the bed, too?"

"I don't know. I hadn't really thought about it." The way she wrapped her hand around the poster and slid it up and down had his thoughts going in a totally different direction. "Do you want me to work my magic on the bed?" he couldn't resist asking.

She rolled her eyes, and than a brief sadness crossed her face. "I guess you wouldn't need to do work on the furniture. Not to sell the house." She smiled brightly. "But things like sprucing up the floors should get you a better price."

"I really hadn't considered that aspect." He shrugged, watching for her reaction when he added, "I don't even know that I'm selling the house yet."

"That's right. You said that, didn't you?" She noisily cleared her throat and walked to the window. "You know, the curtains could use some work. I'm not sure how they'll survive a washing, but if they end up needing some mending I know my way around a sewing machine.''

When he didn't respond she turned to look at him. He just stood there staring at her, a faint smile on his lips.

''What?''

''Nothing.'' He looked away almost as if he had snapped out of a trance. ''Thanks, but I'll probably just get new ones. Blue flowers really aren't to my taste.''

''Oh, yeah, I guess not.'' Carly shrugged, and then crossed her arms over her chest, feeling a little awkward suddenly. ''As long as you don't want anything fancy, the offer still stands. I could sew something like that reasonably well.''

''Thanks. I'll remember that.'' He rubbed his bare chest in a purely male gesture. ''You know if you're still worried about being seen with me, I wouldn't stand near the window like that.'' Amusement danced in his eyes as he purposefully held her gaze. ''I imagine it's fairly easy to see inside.''

She stared at him, her heart starting to pound. Did he know she'd been watching him? No, he couldn't have. It was too dark, and he'd been focused on her parents' house.

Finally, she moved away from the window because he was right, it wouldn't do for anyone to see her in his room.

''There's a lot of really nice woodwork in this house,'' she said, tracing the ornate carving along the edge of the built-in cherry armoire. ''Some of it needs repair but most of it just needs a good polishing. I'm going to be fairly free for the next two weeks before school starts— Why are you looking at me like that?''

''Just trying to figure out if you're offering to help so I'll get the house sold and you'd be rid of me sooner, or if you're thinking I'm not such a bad guy after all and you'd like to hang out with me.''

''You're not such a bad guy, after all.'' She had a teasing light in her eyes that darkened to smoky desire when he started toward her.

''Good answer, Carly Ann Saunders.'' He reached for her hand and she didn't hesitate.

She slid her arms around his waist and tilted her head back for his kiss. He teased her with his tongue, lightly touching her lower lip, trailing to the corner, and then tracing her upper lip.

He left his arms lowered to his sides, his only contact the feather-light touch of his tongue. She closed her eyes and her own arms slackened at his waist. Her body swayed slightly, the sensation making her dizzy.

He touched her nipples and she opened her eyes.

Rick smiled, a lazy sexy smile that did nothing to help stabilize her. Using his index finger, he played with the tightened beads, touching only the very tips. His darkened gaze stayed locked on hers and she couldn't look away.

Didn't want to look away.

The combination of tenderness and raw desire in his eyes was an aphrodisiac all its own. More potent than the most aged wine or the most expensive bottle of brandy, the feeling of being wanted made her feel drunk, heady, other-worldly.

She held her breath, her cotton shirt seeming to

grow thinner beneath his touch. He lightly circled the nipples and then suddenly pinched lightly until she nearly begged him to take her in his mouth. He was trying to drive her crazy and it was working. But it didn't mean she had to play dead. Let him have the upper hand.

Carly touched his fly and he sucked in a breath, his fingers faltering. Drawing the zipper tongue down, she pushed the front of his jeans open.

"I hope you know what you're doing," he whispered hoarsely, and yanked her shirt hem out of her shorts.

"I do." She slid her hands inside his jeans, down his hips, feeling the muscles tense and bunch beneath her palms. The whole thing was heady and liberating because suddenly she knew exactly what she was doing.

God help her, maybe it was love, or maybe simple infatuation, but she was no longer willing to give up another moment she could spend with Rick.

He got to work on her buttons, pressing a kiss to her lips with each one he unfastened. When he finished, he pushed the shirt off her shoulders, glanced briefly at the flesh mounding over the lacy peach bra and then flipped the front clasp and shoved the cups aside.

Staring down at her, his lips slightly parted, he palmed the weight of her breasts in each hand and stared as if totally transfixed. Her nipples were distended so far it was a wonder it wasn't painful.

He lowered his head and flicked out the tip of his tongue. Goose bumps sprang up everywhere, and she shivered. She drew back, and he straightened, his concerned gaze meeting hers. And then she lowered her head and used her tongue to do the same to his nipples.

Groaning, he gripped her hips, pulled her against him, forcing her head up. "Oh, baby, do you have any idea what you do to me?"

Without waiting for an answer, he captured her mouth, his greed for her overriding the earlier tenderness. He plunged his tongue inside her mouth, roaming, exploring until she could no longer breathe.

She finally pulled away and threw back one shoulder and then the other to get rid of the bra. He hungrily suckled her, nearly throwing her off balance. She gripped his shoulders for support, not even realizing that he'd steered her backwards toward the bed. The back of her legs hit the mattress, and then she was lying down and he'd crawled in beside her, his mouth having barely left her breast.

"This isn't enough," he whispered when he finally came up. "I want to taste all of you."

The thought thrilled and unnerved her. New territory for her. Exciting. Scary. But this was Rick. She smiled, happy and content, even as he unzipped her shorts and slid them down her legs. She kicked off her tennis shoes, and he freed her of the shorts. She lay there, completely unself-conscious in peach bikini panties, as he sat back on his haunches and took his time looking her over.

"You're perfect," he whispered, while running his palms over her thighs, her belly, her breasts, and then hooking his fingers in her panties and slowly drawing them down her legs. He tossed the silky fabric on the dresser and then lowered his head.

Unprepared, she tensed. But all he did was kiss the mound of light-brown hair at the juncture of her thighs, and then trailed his tongue up to her navel.

She giggled.

"Did that tickle?" He looked up, grinning.

Carly nodded, and he used his tongue again.

"Knock it off," she said, laughing and trying to squirm away.

"Hey, come back here." He grabbed one of her wrists, half his body landing on top of her. He was hard already. Rock-hard and she wanted him to take off his jeans. She wanted to see him naked. She wanted to feel his hot erect flesh in her hand.

"Your jeans," she whispered, trying to reach in between their bodies.

Keeping her wrist captive, he shifted so that she couldn't touch him. His eyes gleamed with wicked amusement. "What about them?"

"They're still on."

"And?"

"I want them off."

"You do, huh?" He kissed the tip of her nose, her eyelid, and then her mouth. "And what are you going to do once you get them off?"

She hesitated. He was much better at this game than she was. Instead of answering, she licked him across the lips, and when they parted in surprise, she dove in to give him some of his own medicine.

He feverishly kissed her back, letting go of her wrist and struggling out of his jeans. He took his boxers off with them and then lay warm and naked beside her, one of his legs thrown over hers. His erection lay across her belly.

She touched the head and he groaned, tensing against her. A bead of moisture had formed and she used the slickness and her forefinger to explore the sensitive tip. He nearly came off the bed. Capturing her wrist again, he held her hand away from his penis.

"Did I hurt you?" she asked, not really believing she had but looking for reassurance anyway.

His laugh came out raspy and broken. "No." He seemed to have trouble catching his breath. "No, you didn't hurt me."

"Don't you want me to touch you?" She twisted out of his grasp.

"Carly." He tried unsuccessfully to reclaim her hand. "You know this is torture."

"What?"

"Ah, honey..." He groaned when she circled her hand around the base of his shaft. "Wait."

In the split second she hesitated, he had her on her back, her arms stretched out above her head, totally immobile. She stared at the pulse beating fast beneath the tan skin of his throat, keeping time with her own pounding heart.

"What are you doing?" she whispered, excited, not the least afraid.

One side of his mouth curved in a slow, wickedly sexy smile. "What do you want me to do?"

She swallowed. "Everything."

"Be more specific." He moved further back.

"Kiss me."

His lips twitched at the corners, no doubt at her cowardice, but he said nothing. He did as she asked, nibbling gently, drawing her lower lip into his mouth and sucking it, and then exploring with his tongue.

After a very thorough kiss, he lifted his head. "What else? I want to know what you like."

"You haven't figured it out by now?"

He used a gentle hand to brush the hair away from her eyes. "I want you to feel so incredible that you can't live without me."

Her pulse skyrocketed. She didn't know what to say. Scold him for teasing. Pray that he wasn't. "Is this what you brought me up here for? Chitchat?"

He laughed, a low throaty laugh that made her shiver. "Getting a little cocky, huh?"

"Well, I tried but you stopped me."

Rick roared with laughter. "Hey, it's not that little. Okay, don't say you didn't ask for it," he said and buried his face where her neck met her shoulder.

His chin was slightly scratchy and tickly, and she squirmed and giggled and tried to wiggle away. He kept her pinned to the bed while he worked his way down to her breasts. Trailing his tongue around each nipple, he moved his hand to her thighs and coaxed them apart.

She held her breath and fought the instinct to clamp her legs together. He took his time, stroking her gently over her lower belly, lightly touching the cluster of curls that guarded her core.

He slid his fingers between her thighs, playing with the outside of her lips, taunting her ever-blossoming arousal. She moved, trying to take more of his fingers inside her, the sound of her slick wetness driving her crazy.

He jerked away and she whimpered a protest, and then he was kneeling over her, ripping open a foil packet. He handed it to her, and she knew what he wanted her to do, but her hands were shaking too badly.

Finally, with a frustrated growl mixed with laughter, he took it back from her and sheathed himself. He spread her legs further and she realized she'd reflexively closed them. Touching her there again, parting her swollen lips, he gazed at her with such worshipful longing any misgiving melted away. And then he lifted her hips and slid inside her, hard, deep, pushing her to the limit.

She squeezed his shoulders as he pumped harder, every muscle in his body tense and straining. Every time she contracted around him he seemed to push deeper, and when she started to convulse, his cry mingled with hers and he pushed harder still, until she didn't think she could take anymore.

Wave after wave of sensation drenched her with pleasure so intense she thought she'd die from it. She was cold and hot and her limbs boneless. Her brain no longer functioned. It was the most incredible feeling, as if she were falling...falling...but she didn't care. Somehow she knew she'd land safely.

He gave a final cry and slumped over her, although not putting too much weight on her. His body felt more like a warm comfortable blanket that she could snuggle under for the rest of the night.

Bracing himself on one elbow, he brushed the damp

hair away from her face and smiled down at her. "God, Carly, I hope that was even half as good for you as it was for me."

"No contest," she murmured, drowsy with contentment. "You couldn't possibly have felt as wonderful as I did." So much so that it was scary. How could the sex possibly have gotten better?

Maybe because it wasn't sex anymore. Maybe it was love. Oh, God.

His low throaty laugh sent a shiver down her spine. He hugged her to him, rolling over onto his back until she lay on top of him. "Oh, baby, I could just eat you up."

He'd fallen out and she missed the feel of him inside her. She wanted him back inside with a greed that shocked her. She pushed her fingers through his hair and kissed him, hard and demanding, and she felt him stir beneath her.

Drawing back to look at her, he smiled. "Ah, the monster rears its head again."

She tightened her hold of his hair. "What are you going to do about it?"

His eyebrows went up. "Any requests?"

"Surprise me."

Abruptly he rolled her back over, spread her thighs, bent his head down and surprise her he did.

CARLY TURNED over and looked for the clock on her nightstand. It wasn't there. She blinked. She wasn't in her room.

Movement beside her caused her to jerk, and then she remembered. She wiggled closer to Rick, and he put his arm around her, murmured something she couldn't understand and then lapsed into a soft snore.

She smiled and moved her shoulder against his beard-roughened skin. He'd wanted to get up and shave when he'd realized how stubbly his chin had gotten, but she hadn't let him. She hadn't wanted him to be away from her for a single minute. God, she wished she could stay the entire night. But that was impossible.

She stretched to get a look at the digital clock he kept on the dresser. She blinked, hoping the red glowing numbers had tricked her.

Five-twenty.

Panic surged through her. It couldn't be... How could she have slept that long?

She fought the urge to bolt upright. No sense in waking Rick. In fact, she couldn't afford to have him delay her. She had to sneak back to her bedroom. Her father would be awake in an hour.

Quietly, slowly, she turned back the covers and slid her feet to the cold hardwood floor. Rick shifted, extending his arm as if looking for her.

She waited a few seconds for him to settle down, and then bent to kiss him lightly on the mouth. She hoped he understood why she didn't wake him. And why last night could never be repeated. It was all her fault. She accepted full responsibility. Because God help her, she'd fallen in love.

15

"WHAT'S WRONG, Carly? You seem awfully edgy today."

She let go of the curtain, and turned around. She hadn't realized that her mother had entered the kitchen. "I'm not edgy." She shrugged. "Just anxious for school to start."

Her mother tried unsuccessfully to hide a smile. Then, doing an appallingly good job of playing innocent as she tucked her crisp white blouse into her walking shorts, she asked, "What does school have to do with the Weaver house?"

"I have no idea what you're talking about." Carly busied herself with inventorying the refrigerator, silently berating herself for being so obvious. It probably looked as if she was spying on Rick. Which she wasn't. She simply wanted to know if he was awake yet. "Unless you have other plans, I'll make dinner tonight. How does pork roast and sweet potato casserole sound?"

Her mother hesitated long enough that Carly turned around to see what was wrong.

With an apologetic look, her mother took a fresh mug of coffee to the table and said, "Apparently I

forgot to mention it to you. Your father and I won't
be having dinner at home tonight.''

''Oh.''

''But if you still want to make the roast tomorrow
evening that would be great.''

''Sure.'' Carly smiled and got out the orange juice,
wondering where they were going tonight. They almost never went out, unless it was for an occasion like
last week. She didn't know if it was just her, but things
sure seemed weird since she'd come home.

''Maybe you could invite Rick over.''

''When?'' She stared at her mother, eyes widening.

''For dinner tomorrow.''

''Oh. Right.'' She poured her juice, thankful she
had a reason to turn away. God only knew how pink
her face was after that foolish reaction.

''Carly?''

She didn't want to face her. ''Yes,'' she said, finally, as she put the orange juice back in the fridge.

''Something is wrong and I really wish you felt you
could share it with me.''

Carly looked into her mother's troubled eyes.
They'd always been able to talk about anything, and
Carly felt bad that she'd worried her, but it wasn't easy
talking about Rick. Especially not after last night.

The mere memory warmed her all the way down to
her toes. She cleared her throat. ''Don't worry, Mom,
really. I have a lot on my mind. That's all.'' When her
mother looked unconvinced, Carly added, ''The thing
is, part of it concerns a friend so I'm not really at
liberty to discuss the problem with anyone.''

''I see.''

"I know you've heard me mention Ginger."

"The woman you went on vacation with."

Carly nodded. "She's having a small crisis and I feel badly for her."

Her mother's expression softened with understanding. "You're just like your father. Always quick to the rescue."

Carly smiled sheepishly. It wasn't as if she'd lied. She was involved with Ginger's problem and...

Outside, a door slammed.

It had to be Rick. No other house was close enough to be heard.

Carly automatically went to the window and pushed the curtain aside. Rick was putting something in his rental car trunk.

"I have a dentist appointment," she blurted out. "That's where I'll be if I'm not here when you get back." Her mother lifted the mug to her lips. No doubt to conceal a smile. Carly didn't know who she was trying to fool.

Carly scooted out the back door. The route through the backyard was quicker, so she slipped through the hedges, muttering a mild oath when a branch scraped her leg right beneath her denim cutoffs.

Rick looked up from the trunk. Immediately a smile spread across his face. "Good morning."

"Hi." She stopped a few feet away so she didn't do anything stupid like grab him and kiss him. He looked good in khaki cargo shorts and a light-blue T-shirt, snug-fitting from so many washings.

"You sure were quiet this morning," he said softly.

"I left about five-thirty."

"Your parents were asleep, I hope."

She nodded. "They were. I don't think they knew I was gone at all."

"I missed you," he said, taking a step closer, his eyes blazing with purpose.

She tensed, and resisted the urge to look over her shoulder. They were in perfect view if her mother happened to be looking out the window....

"I hadn't expected to fall asleep." She folded her arms across her chest, and she knew she looked defensive when he stopped suddenly. "I had to get home and I figured there was no sense waking you."

"Anyone home at your house now?"

"My mom. She's in the kitchen."

He nodded. "Got it."

She smiled, exceptionally pleased that he was being so understanding. "Are you on your way out?"

"Later I thought I'd go to the hardware store and see if they have any wood repair kits." His gaze roamed her face, lowered to her breasts. "Know what I wanna do to you right now?"

Giddiness bubbled up in her chest and she moistened her lips. "Rick, knock it off."

"I want to lick those pretty pink nipples of yours."

"Oh, God." She briefly looked over her shoulder. She couldn't help it. Of course no one was there.

His slow sexy smile got to her more than his words. "I want to take them in my mouth and suckle them hard."

"If you don't stop it I'm leaving." Dampness gathered between her thighs. "I mean it."

"Stick my tongue in your mouth. Put my finger in—"

"I swear to God I will turn around and go back home if you don't—"

He started to laugh, and she realized she'd pulled her shirt collar away from her warm clammy neck.

"I will get even," she said sweetly. "You'll never see it coming but I will get even."

"I can hardly wait." He had the most beautiful eyes, a mixture of gold and green and sunlight. And, right now, they were suggestive enough she thought it a good idea to sit down.

She heard her mother's car pull out of the garage and wondered if Rick heard it, too. May as well wave the green flag if he had. Going inside was tempting, but awfully dangerous.

"Do you have a few minutes?" she asked.

"For you, anything."

"This is serious. And kind of touchy."

His expression sobered. "Shall we go inside?"

Her gaze drew to the wraparound porch. "How about we sit on the swing?"

"I'm not sure I trust it. That's one of the things I want to repair."

"Really?"

He gave her an odd look.

"I mean, I'd have thought you'd concentrate on the house. I doubt you'd lose a sale over a swing."

His expression darkened, and he gestured for her to precede him. She started to question what she'd said that was so wrong but thought better of it. Probably had nothing to do with her at all. The daunting task of getting the house in shape was enough to dampen anyone's mood.

At least the porch steps were in good shape. She knew that her father, concerned for Mrs. Weaver's safety, had personally seen to that repair about four years ago.

"Is the rocker okay?" she asked, eyeing the weathered cedar chair that had been a fixture of the porch for as long as she could remember.

"We'd be better off in the house."

No one was around, and even so, he was just a neighbor. She took a furtive look around anyway before she pushed the screen door open and went inside.

She didn't get far when Rick came up behind her and slid his arms around her waist. He pulled her against his chest and she readily leaned into him, arching her head back when he kissed the side of her neck.

"This is crazy," she whispered.

"Why? No one's watching." He ran his hands up to her breasts and kneaded them.

She felt him harden against her bottom and she closed her eyes. How was she supposed to think? How was she supposed to ask him about...

"Rick, wait." She moaned when he bit her earlobe. "I have something important to ask you."

He stiffened and then drew back. "Yeah?"

She turned to face him. "It's about Ginger. She wanted me to ask you something."

His eyebrows dipped in a grim frown. "I suppose this has to do with Tony."

Carly hated this, hated being placed in the middle, but she'd foolishly made a promise. "Believe me, this is the last thing I want to do. Besides, I think I already know the answer but I did give Ginger my word that I'd talk to you.''

He shook his head in clear disgust.

''Don't shoot the messenger.''

''It's not you.'' He drew a hand over his face and blew out a breath. ''Tony's a—'' He shook his head again. ''Go ahead. Tell me.''

She sighed. ''Do I really need to spell it out?''

''Did he tell Ginger he'd call?''

''I don't think so. She sort of forced her phone number on him.''

One eyebrow went up. ''I know she's your friend, and I hate to say this, but she knew the score. They had a vacation fling. Tony isn't the for-keeps kind of guy. At least it sounds as if he didn't lead her on.''

''No, he didn't,'' Carly agreed. ''And, frankly, Ginger went on that vacation with the same mindset. But she really liked him and now she's…'' Carly groaned with frustration. ''This was precisely why the anonymity thing was so important.''

''Come on, let's go sit down.'' He took her hand and led her into the living room.

None of the furnishings or rugs or knickknacks had changed over the years. The burgundy velveteen sofa and matching Queen Anne chairs were all still in great shape, probably because Mrs. Weaver seldom used the room.

In the corner, away from the rest of the furniture, was an end table. Made of cherry, she guessed. It was new, much more contemporary than the other pieces.

She stared at it. In fact, it looked as if it might be unfinished.

She pointed to it. "I've never seen that before."

He waved a dismissive hand. "Just a small project of mine. Let's sit on the sofa."

"Wow, it looks really good. Very avant-garde. Did you start from scratch or did you buy the table already constructed?"

"From scratch." He sat down first and pulled her onto his lap. "Who knows? Maybe I've found my true calling. Going from digging up old artifacts to creating futuristic pieces. What a kick, huh?"

She laughed and tried halfheartedly to shift away when he nuzzled her neck. "How are we supposed to talk when you do that?"

"Go ahead, I'm listening." But he kept nibbling and kissing, totally blowing her concentration.

"Rick, darn it, can we please get this conversation over with?"

He did stop then and gave her a sober look. "I don't know what to tell you, except if she's waiting for Tony to call, she can forget it."

"Does he have a girlfriend?"

"No, because he doesn't want one. He enjoys the single life."

"Has he even mentioned Ginger?"

"The truth?"

"Of course."

"Only once, on the way to the airport to fly home. He said he had fun, that it was a great week, but he hoped she wouldn't become a problem."

Carly winced.

He shrugged. "You wanted the truth."

"It's not like I didn't already know this. I just wish Ginger got it." She sighed. "Because guess who has to spell it out for her?"

For the first time since the subject came up he let emotion show. He gave her a sympathetic wink. "Don't let her put you in the middle."

"I'm not. I made it clear that after I talked to you I'd tell her the unvarnished truth and the subject would be dropped."

"Tony's a really great guy. I'd trust him with my life. But he's not the marrying kind."

Are you? She bit her lip to keep from asking the question out loud. Even if he said yes, what difference would it make?

He'd be leaving soon, and she'd committed herself to teaching at the middle school.

He touched the tip of her nose. "What's the frown for?"

"Oh, nothing." She shook her head. "Got sidetracked for a minute."

"Ah. Let me help you get back on track." He kissed her, a gentle coaxing kiss that immediately made her want to beg for more.

He slid his hand up her T-shirt and wasted no time in unclasping her bra. Her nipples were already tight and achy and in desperate need of his touch. He obliged her, kneading and stroking and doing that feather-like flicking that made her insane.

When he pulled the hem of her shirt up, she shot a look toward the front door. He'd closed it.

Rick smiled. "It's locked."

"In Oroville? A locked door? How scandalous."

He chuckled. "I know. Talk about calling attention to ourselves. Maybe I ought to unlock it."

Carly grabbed him by the front of the shirt. "Don't you dare."

"Hmm, I like it when you play rough." He slid his hand down her back and cupped her bottom.

"One of those stop-it-some-more kind of guys, huh?"

He drew back, his eyes lit with surprise. "Carly Ann Saunders, how do you know about such things?"

"I'm going to strangle my mother for blabbing my middle name."

"Worry about that later." He finished taking off her shirt and got rid of her bra.

She stopped him from unsnapping her denim shorts, and then pulled off his shirt. She put her palms on his chest and leisurely rubbed them up and down, loving the feel of his rounded muscles, his excited nipples.

Smiling, she touched her tongue to his right nipple, satisfied when she got an immediate reaction. Both his nipples were quite sensitive but she'd found out last night that the right one had more sensation than the left.

"Hey, hey." He put some distance between them by leaning away from her.

Her smile widened. "I think you're as sensitive there as I am."

"Oh, yeah?" He captured her wrists so she couldn't block him and took one of her nipples into his mouth, his teeth lightly biting as he rapidly flicked his tongue.

She gasped. "Not fair."

He didn't stop, and when she leaned back, he followed her until they both were sprawled across the sofa. While he used one hand to keep both wrists captive, he used the other to unzip her shorts. Laughing, she twisted her body so that he couldn't get them off.

"You're not going to cooperate?" One brow went up, amusement making his eyes golden.

She lifted her chin. "Not until you release my hands."

A slow smile curved his lips. "I don't need your cooperation, honey," he said, and slid a hand under the frayed hem of her shorts.

"What are you— Oh, God." She couldn't breathe. Unerringly, he slid two fingers under the leg of her panties and straight into wet heat. After sliding back and forth a few times, he stroked her swelling clitoris until she arched off the sofa.

"Rick, don't."

"Don't what?" He slid one finger back inside, withdrew and then slid in two. "Don't stop?"

She giggled…moaned…gasped. Heat shot through her. On the verge of orgasm, she closed her eyes.

"You're so beautiful," he whispered. "I want a picture of you just like this with your face flushed and your lips wet and shiny."

She hadn't realized he'd released her wrists until he pulled out his fingers and yanked down her shorts. He spread her thighs, his nostrils flaring as he stared at the wet curls, the swollen nether lips. Then he shucked his own shorts.

He tore open a foil packet he'd retrieved from his pocket. Mesmerized, she watched him sheath himself, amazed at how hard he was. She reached out to touch him, but he moved back, made sure she was ready, and then slid neatly inside her, so deeply she gasped.

She contracted her muscles around him, and he closed his eyes and groaned, the sound so primal, it made her skin tingle.

She could tell he was trying to restrain himself, keeping a slow steady pace. Feeling empowered, she met him with a few thrusts of her own.

He groaned again and pulled himself up, using his hands to brace himself, the muscles of his upper arms bulging and straining with the effort. Looking at her with hooded eyes, his mouth curved in a feral smile. "You're asking for it," he whispered.

"You're right." She lifted her head and tongued his right nipple.

He let out a hoarse cry and came back down on her. He plunged deeper inside, withdrew and then plunged impossibly deeper still. She clung to his shoulders, lifting her pelvis as high as she could, until the spasms came.

They came too soon, with too much potency. She'd wanted to wait, wanted him to come with her, but she flew to the summit of heightened pleasure as each spasm intensified. In the distance she heard him cry her name, and then felt his lips on hers.

A tear spilled and slid down into her hair. She didn't want to open her eyes, fearing this was a dream and that it would all go away. She felt so incredibly right. So well loved.

Love. There it was again. She opened her eyes.

Rick smiled down at her. He kissed the tip of her nose, her chin and then lightly brushed her lips. "Hi."

"Hi back."

"I better warn you." He was still inside her. "I plan on keeping you here all day."

She swallowed. "That sounds wonderful."

He looked serious all of a sudden. "But?"

Apparently something in her voice or expression had given her away. It wasn't possible for her to stay. If she stayed today, or even sneaked back tonight, what about tomorrow? What about next week? Would she end up like Ginger once he returned to his life in California?

The thought was unbearable.

"But," she said sighing, trying hard not to whimper, "I have appointments today."

"Really?"

She nodded, though nearly caving in at his obvious disappointment.

"Shoot. I was hoping you'd go to the hardware store with me. Help me pick out some stuff for the house." He kissed her briefly and then eased off her.

He was still a little hard and she had to force her gaze away. As naturally as if they did it every day, he pulled her to a sitting position and then urged her onto his lap again.

She leaned back against him and he crossed his arms over her chest, each hand palming a breast. "Were you serious about finding a new calling?" she asked.

"I don't know. Just talking."

Disappointment dampened her spirits. "When are you going back to Los Angeles?"

His entire body tensed. "Why?"

It wasn't her imagination. Even his hands slackened on her breasts. Did he think she was pulling a Ginger? That she'd beg him to stay? "I was just wondering how much time you'd have to do all this work around the house you've been talking about."

He relaxed a little. "I honestly don't know. I'm in the middle of a research project. I've been working on a report from my laptop and e-mailing the information every other day. But I guess I'll have to show up in my office before school starts."

"School?"

"I work for a university."

She twisted around to look at him. "You didn't tell me."

"Research is research. Where does it matter where I do it or for whom?"

"Why do you sound so defensive?" She touched his cheek. "I was just curious."

"I just didn't want you to think—" He shrugged, a self-deprecating smile lifting one side of his mouth. "You know the old saying, those who can't do, teach."

His callousness stung. "No, I guess I haven't heard that one."

"Oh, shit." He tightened his arms around her. "Carly, I'm sorry. I didn't mean you. It's different in archeology. It's just— Don't be angry. I'm sorry."

"No problem." She sighed, trying not to take offense, and glanced at her watch. "I have to go."

"You are mad."

She got up and gathered her clothes. "No, really, the timing is rotten, that's all. I've stayed too long as it is."

"Right. You have appointments." He watched with a hungry gaze as she pulled on her panties and shorts.

"I do," she said, and gave him a parting kiss.

She wasn't mad. Hurt, yes, but also grateful. They came from different worlds, and had made very different choices. She'd needed the reminder.

16

CARLY REVERSED her Honda down the drive and onto the street, and then shot another glance at Rick's house before heading toward town. Stupid, because she knew he wasn't home. His car had been gone all day.

She'd studied tons of psychology and she'd even volunteered as a counselor while she was at the university. But she'd never truly understood the power of addiction, or more accurately, the powerlessness of addiction.

For two days she'd suffered major Rick withdrawal. She'd seen him twice from her bedroom window leaving early in the morning, and once from the kitchen while she was making dinner last night. She'd thought about giving in and sneaking over, but he'd left again before they'd finished eating.

Carly didn't think he was actually avoiding her because he had stopped by when she wasn't home yesterday. Her mother had answered the door and had him in for a cup of coffee. The idea made Carly nervous, but apparently all they'd discussed was what type of flowers to plant in the fall.

Even when she wasn't with him he made her crazy. Why would he care about fall flowers? He wouldn't be here. He'd be back in California, and Carly would be here in Oroville, teaching, just as she'd always wanted to do. And she'd be miserable. Because she'd foolishly fallen in love with Rick.

She couldn't even be angry with him. It was her fault. She'd known the risk. And she'd proceeded without caution.

A car horn blasted, and she jumped.

Her heart still somersaulting, she steered her Honda to the curb.

She'd run a stop sign that had been on that same corner her entire life. Totally absorbed in her thoughts, she hadn't noticed it. She made sure she was legally parked and got out of the car. Her grocery list would have to wait.

She checked her watch. Oroville's only movie theatre showed movies that were six months old, and whatever was playing this afternoon she'd probably already seen, but she didn't care. It was the perfect place to hide out, eat copious amounts of buttered popcorn and not think how hard it was to sleep at night without dreaming of *him*.

"Hi ya, Carly. Long time no see." Bonnie Gibson stood behind the candy counter grinning.

She and her husband owned and operated the small theatre that had been in her family for two generations. That they owned the land and building was probably the only reason they could afford to stay open; that and the fact that they rented out videos, too.

"Hi, Bonnie." Carly reached into her purse. "One ticket and one tub of popcorn, extra butter."

"Are you by yourself?" Bonnie asked, craning her neck to see outside the window. She was only about seven years older than Carly but she acted like an old lady sometimes.

"Yep. Add a diet cola and a package of M&M's to that, would you, please?"

"Girl, you can't eat all of that by yourself."

Carly sighed. "I'm sure gonna try." She glanced at her watch, trying to give Bonnie the hint to hurry up.

Shaking her head, the woman filled up a tub of popcorn and squirted on a ton of butter. She had trouble with the squirt gun from the soda machine but finally managed to top off a medium cup, and then she pulled a pencil out of her ever-present ponytail and scratched something on a piece of paper.

She turned the paper around to show Carly a figure. "Does that total look about right to you?"

"You forgot the M&M's." Carly laid the money on the counter.

Bonnie frowned, and Carly didn't miss the quick glance Bonnie gave her stomach. Probably thought Carly was pregnant. "If you don't open them you can bring them back for a refund," Bonnie said as she handed over the bag.

"Thanks." Without waiting for the few cents change, Carly gathered up her goodies and went into the already dark theater.

She smiled. This was probably the last theater in America that still showed cartoons before the main attraction. They were always awful, the really old ones that she hadn't liked even when she was a kid. But today, as she settled into the same middle seat she always claimed, the silly cartoon provided an odd sort of comfort.

She sat back, dug into her popcorn and tried not to think about Rick. It was kind of sad to see only a dozen other heads in the place. With so many people going to Cedar City for their groceries and entertainment, she didn't see how the Gibsons could continue to stay in business. The handwriting was on the wall. Eventually they'd become another casualty of progress and big business.

Why would Oroville stay the same just because Carly Saunders wanted it to? It bothered her to see so many changes, even in her parents' routine. They went out more and the nightly 'family dinner' was no longer sacred.

So why had she come back? Everything was bound to change eventually.

No. She wasn't going to do that. Start rationalizing reasons to leave Oroville. To follow Rick. She wouldn't be another Ginger. Never. Not in this lifetime. Besides, he hadn't once said he wanted her to be with him.

The cartoon ended and the theater got dark again. Someone had just walked in, and paused at the end of her aisle. Just what she needed…someone sitting nearby. But the place was empty, plenty of seats down the middle in front and in back of her. No one in their right mind would crowd in.

Her attention drew to the preview of what would be coming to Oroville next week. She shook her head. She'd bet the rest of her popcorn that all the kids in town had seen this movie in Cedar City already. An excellent bet to lose, though, knowing she'd regret all this popcorn. She reached into the tub for another buttery handful.

Instead, she found another hand.

She jumped, throwing the popcorn container in the air.

Rick caught it.

She put a hand to her throat. "What the heck are you doing here?"

Someone from behind shushed her. Carly cringed.

"You almost dumped our popcorn," he whispered and then shoved a handful into his mouth.

"Our?"

"Pass me the cola." He put out his free hand. "Did you add extra salt to this?"

She gave him the drink and, remembering to keep her voice low, said, "You can't keep popping up like this, unannounced, uninvited."

"That's the thing...I knew you would have asked me to come if we hadn't kept missing each other."

"Missing each other? You've hardly made an effort—" She cut herself off, irritated with herself at what she'd been about to admit, and then glanced around to see if anyone was listening.

He leaned over, his mouth close to her ear, and whispered, "I thought you'd be pleased at my discretion."

His spicy scent infused her senses, intoxicated her. "What do you mean?"

"Staying in the shadows as I have."

"What are you talking about?" she asked, not liking the way he sounded suddenly, tense and slightly mocking.

"Aren't I your dirty little secret? Isn't that where you want to keep me, in the shadows?"

She sat up in her seat and swung her head to put him in his place. But not wanting to make a scene, she settled back into her seat. "I never said that," she murmured quietly. "What's wrong with you, anyway? Have you been drinking?"

"You know better."

She sighed. "You don't understand, Rick."

"Apparently, neither do you. Did you think I came back just to get laid? I could do that in L.A., easy."

She moistened her lips, her mind starting to race, not sure what he was saying.

"You think I don't see the way you look around to make sure no one is watching you associate with an undesirable like me? You think that doesn't hurt?"

"Undesirable? That's ridiculous. This has nothing to do with you personally."

"I don't know how much more personal we could get."

From behind, someone told them to quiet down.

Of course the person was right, and, embarrassed, Carly abruptly stood. Surprising Rick, she managed to slip by, then headed down the aisle and out to the theater lobby. Thankfully, she saw that Bonnie was bending down behind the counter organizing the candy shelf and didn't notice as Carly hurried by and entered the restroom.

She'd have rather gotten in her car and driven off, but her purse and keys were still sitting on the seat. She wasn't worried about retrieving them. They were safe enough, but darn she wished she could be out of here. At home. Locked in her room.

The bathroom consisted of one sink and two stalls, both of which were empty, thank goodness. She went to the sink and splashed cold water on her face, and then looked at her reflection in the mirror.

She still looked the same. So why was she acting like such a dope? She could spout off all she wanted about Rick and her having no future together, but deep down the hope hadn't died. She knew better, darn it. She should never have slept with him.

Carly heard someone at the door and she quickly dabbed at her eyes, checked out her red nose. She hadn't exactly been crying but...

"Carly?"

Rick. She spun around. "What are you—? You can't be in here. You—you—get out."

"I'm not leaving until we talk."

"About what?"

"Us."

"Don't worry. I'm not like Ginger." She tried not to cringe at the lie. "I understand totally."

"Well, I don't understand at all. Why don't you clue me in?"

"Rick, please. I live here. I have to face these people every day. Your bag is probably already packed, your passport sitting on top ready for you to take off."

"Don't be so sure," he said quietly.

She stared at him. He looked so glum. "What do you mean?"

"Who said I'm leaving?"

"Well, there obviously isn't much need for an archeologist around here.'' Not to mention he'd be bored out of his mind in a month.

He shrugged, and looked away.

"Rick, all you ever talked about was following in your parents' footsteps."

"I was a kid. Not everyone knows what they want at that age. You were lucky. You knew without reservation and you went after it."

Her heart raced. "But you like the research part…"

He shrugged again. "Yeah."

Maybe he hadn't been fixing up his grandmother's house just to sell it. Carly swallowed around the lump in her throat. "You realize that teaching and research can go hand-in-hand."

"Teaching?" He drew his head back, the look of disgust on his face taking her aback.

She tried not to get defensive. Tried really hard. "I know what you've said about it—"

"Look, I'm a doer, not a teacher, okay?"

"Fine. I just thought that if you wanted to stay in Oroville—"

"I don't know that I'm staying. I don't know what I'm going to do."

Carly stared, dumbfounded. One minute he seemed uncertain and vulnerable, and she felt badly for him. The next minute he was a jerk. Had he been toying with her? She didn't want to think he could be that cruel.

She heard someone at the door. As it opened, Carly suddenly remembered where they were standing.

With the help of her wooden cane, Gerdie Hopkins walked in. She smiled at Carly, and then saw Rick and screamed.

RICK STOOD BACK to look at the table he'd just finished varnishing. He hated to make another trip to Cedar City today but he needed a finer grade of sandpaper before he applied the final coat. He was learning, slowly, and with minimal frustration. Besides, what else did he have to do?

After the scene in the theater yesterday, he doubted Carly had much to say to him. With good reason. He'd been a jerk. Worse, he'd sounded like his elitist parents. What the hell did they know anyway?

They couldn't even keep their marriage together. Sure, people got divorced all the time, but generally not over who should have top billing for the latest find. And raising a son? Forget about it. They didn't know a thing about that either. What the hell had ever made him think he wanted to be like them?

He washed his paintbrush and stored his tools and then went to the window and stared out toward Carly's bedroom. She had to be really be pissed. Not that he blamed her. He was pretty pissed at himself, too. How could he have belittled her profession like that? Why hadn't she slapped him the first time he'd made the stupid remark about teaching?

He cringed just thinking about his thoughtless remarks. Pure pride and jealousy had driven him. She seemed to have it together, knowing exactly what she wanted and going after it with unwavering determination. Not like him. Pushing thirty and all he had was a job, not a career. Research paid the bills. But there was no passion in his soul.

Well, that wasn't entirely true. He did like the research aspect. Ironically it was the field work that had lost its appeal.

So what? He didn't have to stick to an adolescent fantasy. Lots of kids wanted to be firemen or policemen or doctors, but that didn't mean that's how they ended up as adults. Somewhere in the back of his mind he'd convinced himself that anything besides the thrill of the dig was substandard, average at best. Tediously average. God forbid.

Carly wasn't average. Her job could be considered common but that didn't make her average. She was smart and adventurous and gutsy, and she'd provided him with some of the best memories of his life. Her and Gram. When could he say he'd had a better time? Felt more like he belonged? Felt wanted?

He sighed and leaned against the windowsill. The pressure caused some of the white paint to crack along the frame. He studied the seal, and realized it also needed some work. A house this age was hardly energy-efficient and if he was going to stay, he really had to...

The thought stopped him.

He took a deep breath and gazed off toward Carly's house again. Of course, the idea of sticking around had flitted through his mind a couple of times. In fact, he should have headed back to L.A. by now. But the thought of actually putting down roots...

Man, that would be something. A real home. Carly. A couple of kids. One of those minivans to cart them and their friends to soccer games.

Shit, he was going off the deep end. Carly wasn't even speaking to him. Not that he truly knew what the hell he wanted to do with his life yet. With his career, anyway. It was turning out that he was pretty good at woodwork. Maybe he could parlay that into some kind of occupation. But what?

Teaching?

He chuckled out loud. Now, there was a concept. Him, a teacher. Of course woodworking was pretty hands-on. That would be different. The idea wasn't without merit. Although there was that thing about eating crow.

He muttered a curse. How did he get so screwed up? All his life he'd thought he knew exactly where and how he'd end up. He stared at Carly's window again. He knew he wanted her. As his partner. His wife. The mother of his children. He'd never met anyone more loyal. More loving. Caring. Focused. Someone who made him want to get off his ass and do something besides feel sorry for himself.

Briefly he closed his eyes and smiled humorlessly at himself. She wasn't ashamed to be with him as he'd thought. That was his own bruised ego, his own insecurity creating doubt. As she'd once told him, it wasn't all about him. She'd merely been protecting herself. She loved Oroville and she knew what she wanted. Couldn't fault her for that.

Outside he heard a car door slam and he leaned over further to see if it was Carly. Another chunk of paint fell to the floor.

Man, so much work had to be done to the house. Almost as much as it would take to win Carly. If he were half the man he wanted to be, he'd prevail. He had no choice. That was the kind of man Carly deserved.

17

CARLY SAT at her window seat and stared at the moon.
It was beautiful, so serene, so surreal with its glowing
halo. She tried not to think about the last time she'd
admired its beauty. At the lake. With Rick.

Her gaze automatically went back to Mrs. Weaver's
house. No, Rick's house. It was his now. For however
long he decided to hold on to it.

Three-thirty, and the downstairs light was still on.
Not because it had been forgotten. She was quite certain she'd seen his shadow a couple of times. Maybe
he was doing some of the woodwork he seemed to
enjoy.

Now that she'd had a couple of days to cool off and
weather the sting of his remarks about her profession,
she was truly glad he had embraced his new hobby
with such passion. Twice in the past three days she'd
seen him unload his car after a trip to the hardware
store, and yesterday evening when she'd left her window open, she'd heard him pounding.

Sighing, Carly briefly, foolishly thought about going
over and knocking on his door. As the hurt had started
to ebb, sympathy mounted. He had to feel pretty lost.
As kids they'd both been certain about which paths
they wanted to take. True, most kids change their

minds several times before they choose a career. But not her and Rick. She was going to be a teacher and he was going to be an archeologist. Period.

While lying in bed the past two nights, she recalled the conversations they'd had about their futures. Hers had been a quiet steady conviction, while his had been a passionate determination to be as great as his parents. How awful it had to be for him to suddenly feel rudderless.

Maybe that's why he'd hung on to his grandmother's house, a source of warm memories, familiarity. It gave him roots he'd never really had. Temporarily, anyway. Because sooner or later he'd find another path, another passion, or maybe even rekindle his love for archeology and he'd be off in hot pursuit.

Selfishly, Carly didn't want to think about that. Except she did want him to be happy, and right now he probably could use a friend. Tomorrow, she promised herself, she'd swallow her pride and go see Rick.

And try to forget that she'd fallen foolishly, hopelessly in love with him.

It was still early when the phone rang. Carly hadn't opened her eyes yet. It had to be one of her father's parishioners. When no one picked it up, she rolled over and fumbled for the receiver sitting on her nightstand.

As she answered and noticed the clock beside it, her eyes opened plenty. Ten-thirty? She never slept that late. Never.

"Carly?" It was Ginger.

Great. Carly fell back into the pillows. "Yep, it's me."

"Did I wake you?"

"No." She yawned and covered the phone.

"Are you okay?"

"Why wouldn't I be?" She blinked at the clock. Nothing changed. It really was ten-thirty. Her father was at the church office and her mother volunteered at the community center today.

Ginger didn't answer at first. Finally, she said. "I assume Rick is still there."

"Look, Ginger, I thought we agreed. No more talk about Tony."

"I know. I'm not calling about him. To tell you the truth, I hadn't even thought about him for days. Not much, anyway." She laughed softly. "I was calling about Rick."

Any residual grogginess faded and Carly sat up. "What about him?"

"Why is he still there?"

"I honestly don't know." Carly frowned. "Why the concern?"

"I'm worried about you."

"Me?" Carly laughed around a yawn. She glanced at the clock again. In two hours she had an appointment with the principal.

"Yeah, you. How are you holding up?"

"I should be asking you."

"Nope. I wasn't in love with Tony. Just infatuated."

"You're not saying that I—" Carly's chest tightened and she sat up straighter. "Whatever gave you that idea?"

"Please."

"I'm serious. If you recall, I was the one who thought getting together with him was a bad idea."

"Does the phrase 'the lady doth protest too much' have any significance for you?"

Carly snorted. "I simply didn't want to end up pining away like you."

"Ouch! That smarted."

"Sorry, I shouldn't have said that."

"That's okay. I deserved it after the way I've acted." Ginger paused. "Are you sure Tony—" She sighed. "Never mind. Okay, let's cut the bullshit. What's going on with Rick?"

"Nothing. I swear."

"Is he selling his grandmother's house?"

"He doesn't know yet."

After a lengthy pause, Ginger asked, "If not, what is he going to do with it?"

"I don't know."

"Come on, Carly."

"I honestly don't know." She combed her fingers through her hair, amazed at how tangled the short strands could get.

"Look, I have an appointment with the principal from my new school this afternoon and I still haven't showered yet."

"Okay, I understand. But do me a favor. Talk to him."

The temptation to play dumb was great, but where would it get her. "I will."

"I mean it, Carly. I don't want you to blow it because you're too stubborn to admit it's possible you two could work things out."

"Right." She liked it better when Ginger was too miserable about her own affairs to butt into Carly's.

"Be as condescending as you want, but you obviously didn't see the way he looked at you," Ginger said. "Go for it, girlfriend. Or I swear you'll live to regret it." She hung up before Carly could tell her she was crazy.

CONSIDERING SCHOOL didn't start for another week, the corridor was abuzz with excitement and activity. Classroom windows and doors were open and a nice breeze blew through, easing the late August temperature.

Of course it was never really hot in Oroville. When it got up to the mid-eighties, people complained about sweltering. Half of them would never have survived that week in the Caribbean.

Carly sighed with disgust. Why did everything have to remind her of that fateful week in the Caribbean? And Rick? And how messed up her life had gotten?

Two little girls she recognized but couldn't name waved, and she smiled and waved back. They were about eleven or twelve, which meant they'd probably be in her class.

It wasn't too late, she decided. With school starting she'd have so much to think about and lessons to plan, papers to grade. All the things Rick said he'd hate to do as a teacher.

Darn it! She was not going to think about him.

She took a deep breath and opened the door to Mr. Shirley's office.

"Hey, Carly." Lou Ann Godfrey, the principal's secretary, looked up from her desk in the reception area. "Nice to see you back."

"Thanks. I heard you had twins. You look great."

Lou Ann gave her a wry smile. "Twin monsters. I love them to pieces but I've never been so glad to be working in my entire life. My mom keeps them during the day, bless her heart."

A wave of wistfulness swept Carly. She had no idea where it came from. She loved kids but really hadn't thought much about having them yet. She inclined her head toward Mr. Shirley's closed door. "I have an appointment with him."

"Yeah, I know. He's got someone in there now but I'm sure they're just about done. Mind having a seat? We have coffee if you'd like."

"No, thanks." Carly sat in one of the visitors' chairs and tugged down the hem of her navy-blue skirt. This was just an informal meeting about the new interactive curriculum she wanted to try out, but she'd decided to stick to more professional attire.

While she waited she flipped through her notes, rehearsing the pitch she'd planned in her head. The favorable statistics she'd collected spoke highly of the program that had been implemented in several urban schools. She'd use them if she couldn't convince Mr. Shirley that it was worth the effort simply on the merit of the program itself.

Out of the blue, she heard Rick's distinctive husky laughter.

She looked up from her notes. Lou Ann typed away at her computer.

Carly blinked. Great. Now she was imagining things.

She went back to her notes and heard the laugh again. Her head came up, her gaze drawing to Mr. Shirley's closed door. No, it couldn't be...

Lou Ann stopped typing and smiled. "I sure hope he hires him."

"Excuse me?"

"The new guy Mr. Shirley is interviewing. He's gorgeous, and God knows we could use the eye candy around here." Lou Ann giggled. "And if you tell my husband I said that I'll deny it till my dying breath."

"Please tell me that isn't Rick Baxter in there."

Lou Ann wrinkled her nose. "I believe that's his name." She peered at her desk calendar. "Yup, that's him."

The office door opened, and Rick stepped out first, his back to Carly. Mr. Shirley came out right behind him and extended a hand.

Numb with shock, Carly stared. What the hell was Rick doing? He wasn't looking for a teaching job. He had no business here. Hadn't he ruined enough of her life?

"Good talking to you, Rick. I feel certain we can work something out." Mr. Shirley pumped Rick's hand. "Too bad we didn't talk a month ago."

"I know." Rick had on gray slacks, a crisp white dress shirt. "I appreciate you working with me on this."

"No problem. I'll be in touch." Mr. Shirley looked

past him at Carly. "Sorry, to keep you waiting, Carly. Mind giving me two more minutes?"

Slowly Rick turned around, a surprised look on his face.

"Of course not," she mumbled, trying to regain her composure, trying not to let her hands shake.

Through the glass, she watched Mr. Shirley hurry down the hall toward the restroom. His timing couldn't have been better. She needed the space to regroup her thoughts so she didn't make a total jackass of herself.

"You were my next stop." Rick had moved to stand in front of her, blocking her view of Lou Ann.

She didn't want the woman overhearing anything they had to say. "Let's talk later."

"We have two minutes. I only need one." His lips curved in that sexy, heart-stopping smile that had the power to cut her off at the knees.

She stood, hoping her legs held out. "Let's go for a walk. Lou Ann, I'll be back in a minute," she said, without looking at the other woman as she led Rick out of the office.

They got outside and she turned around to ask him what the heck he was doing but before she could open her mouth, he kissed her.

She drew back before she got so tangled in his web she wouldn't be able to think straight. He put a finger to her lips.

"Me first," he said, his gaze locked on hers. "I love you, Carly Ann Saunders."

She stared at him. "You do?"

He nodded his head, a flicker of fear mixed with

uncertainty in his eyes, the display of vulnerability squeezing her heart.

''Are you sure?''

That startled a laugh out of him. ''I'm sure.''

''Good.'' She swallowed. ''Because I love you, too.''

''You sure?''

She nodded, laughed, hiccupped. ''Positive.''

He slid his arms around her waist. ''What are we going to do about it?''

Her heart thudded as she tilted her head back to look at him. ''Any ideas?''

''One.''

''Oh?''

His gaze went over her head and noticed a few teachers looking at them. ''Uh-oh. We have an audience.''

''The heck with them.'' She didn't even turn around. ''What's your idea?''

He grinned. ''I know it sounds so traditional, and awfully old-fashioned but...'' He paused.

''What?''

''Ouch!'' He jerked when she lightly pinched his shoulder.

''What? Darn it.''

''Will you marry me?''

She swallowed. Her mouth was so dry that it hurt. ''What about your job? Your place in L.A.?'' She held her breath, half expecting him to laugh. Tell her he had no intention of living in Oroville. That he expected her to move.

''I have a place here. With you. If you'll let me.''

She forced herself to remain calm. "It's a different lifestyle here."

He nodded solemnly. "I know that."

"What will you do?"

"I hope I'll teach here with you." He gave her a mock glare. "No 'I-told-you-sos,' but I was thinking that I'm not half bad working with wood and I know a lot about coaching football, so I figured it was worth a shot to talk to—"

Raising herself on the tip of her toes, she kissed him. "Yes," she said finally. "Yes, I want to spend my life with you."

He kissed her again, ignoring the cheers and whistles from the sidelines.

Epilogue

"CARLY ANN BAXTER, I swear I'll be a hundred before you make me a grandmother." Eileen Saunders said as she took the squirming puppy from Carly. "I should be watching your children, not your cocker spaniel. Do you want me to feed him once or twice a day?"

Carly smiled at her mom's impatience. Carly and Rick had only been married for two years and this was the second time her mom had commented on their childless state. "Twice, but give him only half as much the second time."

"Honey, do you have our passports?" Rick came down the hall, his feet still bare even though they had a plane to catch in two hours. "Hi, Mom. Thanks for watching Buddy for us."

"I should be watching grandchildren," she muttered again, giving Carly a significant look.

Rick chuckled. "We're working on it."

"Are you really?"

Carly gave him a warning glare. She didn't want anyone to know yet. Especially not her impatient mother.

"Maybe you'll have good news when you come back from Egypt," her mom said, nearly losing

Buddy. Once the dog saw Rick, he wanted down. Not that Rick spoiled him rotten or anything.

"Maybe," Carly said, picking up a piece of paper, folding it and tucking it into her mom's pocket. "Here's information on how you can reach us if you need to. It's the Western Union office in Cairo."

Her mom nodded. This was their second dig so she understood they'd be camping out in the middle of nowhere.

"You'd better hurry," she said, glancing at the kitchen clock, and then kissing them both on the cheek before moving toward the back door. "And don't worry about your plants. I'll come over twice a week and water them."

"Thanks, Mom," they both said in unison.

As soon as she disappeared, Rick grabbed Carly around the waist and swung her around to face him.

"Don't start," she warned, laughing when he nuzzled her neck. "You aren't even ready and we've got to drive to Cedar City yet."

"You're right." He kissed her briefly. "I'll be ready in five. You have the passports?"

She nodded and then watched him go back down the hall. Could they possibly be any happier? She didn't think so. Teaching together during the school year, and going to exotic places for the summer so he could keep up with his research publishing.

Carly sighed. It didn't get any better than this.

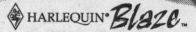

HARLEQUIN® *Blaze*™

In L.A., nothing remains confidential for long…

KISS & TELL

Don't miss

Tori Carrington's

exciting new miniseries featuring four
twentysomething friends—
and the secrets they *don't* keep.

Look for:

#105—NIGHT FEVER
October 2003

#109—FLAVOR OF THE MONTH
November 2003

#113—JUST BETWEEN US…
December 2003

Available wherever Harlequin books are sold.

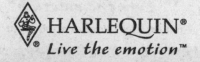

HARLEQUIN®
Live the emotion™

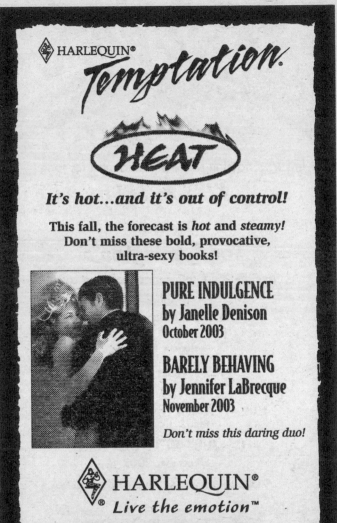

If you enjoyed what you just read,
then we've got an offer you can't resist!

Take 2 bestselling
love stories FREE!
Plus get a FREE surprise gift!

Clip this page and mail it to Harlequin Reader Service®

IN U.S.A.	IN CANADA
3010 Walden Ave.	P.O. Box 609
P.O. Box 1867	Fort Erie, Ontario
Buffalo, N.Y. 14240-1867	L2A 5X3

YES! Please send me 2 free Blaze™ novels and my free surprise gift. After receiving them, if I don't wish to receive anymore, I can return the shipping statement marked cancel. If I don't cancel, I will receive 4 brand-new novels each month, before they're available in stores! In the U.S.A., bill me at the bargain price of $3.80 plus 25¢ shipping and handling per book and applicable sales tax, if any*. In Canada, bill me at the bargain price of $4.21 plus 25¢ shipping and handling per book and applicable taxes**. That's the complete price and a savings of at least 10% off the cover prices—what a great deal! I understand that accepting the 2 free books and gift places me under no obligation ever to buy any books. I can always return a shipment and cancel at any time. Even if I never buy another book from Harlequin, the 2 free books and gift are mine to keep forever.

150 HDN DNWD
350 HDN DNWE

Name	(PLEASE PRINT)	
Address	Apt.#	
City	State/Prov.	Zip/Postal Code

* Terms and prices subject to change without notice. Sales tax applicable in N.Y.
** Canadian residents will be charged applicable provincial taxes and GST.
  All orders subject to approval. Offer limited to one per household and not valid to
  current Blaze™ subscribers.
  ® are registered trademarks of Harlequin Enterprises Limited.

BLZ02-R

HARLEQUIN® *Blaze*™

HARLEQUIN® *Temptation.*

Single in South Beach

Nightlife on the Strip just got a little hotter!

Join author Joanne Rock as she takes you to Miami Beach and its hottest new singles playground. Club Paradise has opened for business and the women in charge are determined to succeed at all costs. So what will they do with the sexy men who show up at the club?

SEX & THE SINGLE GIRL
Harlequin Blaze #104
September 2003

GIRL'S GUIDE TO HUNTING & KISSING
Harlequin Blaze #108
October 2003

ONE NAUGHTY NIGHT
Harlequin Temptation #951
November 2003

Don't miss these red-hot stories from Joanne Rock!
Watch for the sizzling nightlife to continue in spring 2004.

Look for these books at your favorite retail outlet.

Visit us at www.eHarlequin.com